Publisher:
John Betancourt

Editor:
Robert M. Price

Managing Editor:
Sean Wallace

Distribution Manager:
Abner Gibber.

Strange Tales is published quarterly by Wildside Press LLC, P.O. Box 301, Holicong, PA 18928-0301. Postmaster & others: send change of address and other subscription matters to Wildside Press, attn: *Strange Tales*, P.O. Box 301, Holicong, PA 18928-0301. Single copies: $7.50 (magazine edition), postage included in the U.S.A. Add $2.00 per copy for shipping elsewhere. Subscriptions: 4 issues for $19.95 in the U.S.A. and its possessions, $29.95 in Canada, and $39.95 elsewhere. All payments must be in U.S. funds and drawn on a U.S. financial institution. If you wish to use PayPal to pay for your subscription, email your payment to: wildside@sff.net.

Tell us what you think! Visit the official *Strange Tales* message board at:

www.wildsidepress.com

You can also drop us a line at:

Wildside Press
P.O. Box 301
Holicong, PA 18928–0301
www.wildsidepress.com

We invite letters of comment (via email or regular mail), and we assume all letters received are intended for publication (unless marked "Do Not Publish") and become the property of Wildside Press, LLC.

Fiction and poetry submissions: Authors may submit work to the editor. Please query first to insure that the editor is currently reading new submsisions. Queries to: criticus@aol.com..

Art submissions: Please email wildsidepress@yahoo.com.

STRANGE TALES OF MYSTERY AND TERROR   **VOL. 4, NO. 2**

Contents

THE BELFRY

by Robert M. Price

Some readers, upon hearing of a periodical called *Strange Tales*, may think first of the wonderful early 1960s Marvel Comics magazine featuring brief tales of science fiction and fantasy written by Stan Lee and drawn by the likes of Steve Ditko, Jack Kirby, Don Heck, and Larry Leiber. This anthology format was followed, in the wake of the success of the Lee-Kirby *Fantastic Four*, with a monthly comic divided between the Human Torch (in an attempt to provide him a solo career like his Golden Age namesake) and the Thing on the one hand, and Dr. Strange, master of the mystic arts, on the other. Dr. Strange's strip, however, was a true though unannounced harking back to something even before the Timely Comics Human Torch, namely the short-lived rival to *Weird Tales*, the pulp magainze *Strange Tales of Mystery and Terror.*

Strange Tales was published by the Clayton Magazines group, publisher also of *Astounding Stories* (today reduced to the mundane *Analog Science Fact / Science Fiction*), *Ace-High Magazine, Ranch Romances, Cowboy Stories*, and several others. William Clayton just hated to see blank space going to waste on the huge proof sheets for the covers of the company's many monthly pulps. And so his stable grew as he cooked up new titles to take up that space! The first expansion title was, in fact, *Astounding Stories* (as of January, 1930), followed by *Strange Tales* in September of the following year. *Astounding Stories* editor Harry Bates proposed its weird fiction counterpart to fill another hole because he couldn't help noticing the success of Popular Publications' *Weird Tales.* Surely there was room in the market for another like it! All the more since Bates was already working with a number of the prominent *Weird Tales* scribes in the pages of *Astounding*, including the great names of Jack Williamson, Hugh B. Cave, Paul Ernst, and Edmond Hamilton. Surely these gents must have more fiction in their files than *Weird Tales* could accommodate? And indeed they did!

Weird Tales authors including Robert E. Howard, Frank Belknap Long, and Clark Ashton Smith rejoiced at the birth of a new market, and at the chance to run stories rejected by the editorial caprice of *Weird Tales* by editor Bates, who was of course only too happy to get them! H.P. Lovecraft resisted the temptation, as he explained to *Weird Tales* editor Farnsworth Wright: "You may recall that I wouldn't contribute to *Strange Tales* because Bates couldn't guarantee me immunity from the copy-slasher's shears and blue pencil" (February 16, 1933). Ironically enough, Lovecraft had already snuck into Bates's pages; he ghostwrote the major portion of "The Trap" for his friend Henry S. Whitehead! It appeared in the March, 1932 issue.

Today we are inclined to see *Strange Tales* (as well as another copycat, *Strange Stories*) as equally venerable colleagues of the legendary *Weird Tales*. In fact, just as Henry Kuttner might appear in *Strange Stories* under the pseudonym Will Garth, or Robert Bloch as Tarleton Fiske, *Strange Tales* might as well have been a moonlighting pen name for *Weird Tales*!

Many great pulp horror and fantasy tales appeared between the covers of the mere seven issues of *Strange Tales*, including "Murgunstrum" (January, 1933) and "Stragella" (June, 1932) by Hugh B. Cave; "People of the Dark" (June, 1932) and "The Cairn on the Headland" (January, 1933) by Robert E. Howard; "Wolves of Darkness" (January,

BACK ISSUES AVAILABLE!

When *Strange Tales* first appeared in 1931 as a pulp magazine, it was clearly something new. Edited by Harry Bates as a companion to *Astounding Stories*, it combined the supernatural horror and fantasy of *Weird Tales* with vigorous action plots. Had the Great Depression not intervened and killed it after seven issues, the whole history of fantastic fiction might have been different. *Strange Tales* rapidly attracted the most imaginative and capable writers of the day, including Robert E. Howard, Clark Ashton Smith, Henry S. Whitehead, Hugh B. Cave, Jack Williamson, August Derleth, Ray Cummings, and numerous others. Classics from its pages include Williamson's "Wolves of Darkness," and Derleth's Cthulhu Mythos tale, "The Thing That Walked on the Wind." Certainly *Strange Tales* gave *Weird Tales* a serious run for its money.

We have 2 back issues available: a facsimile reprint of the original #7 (January 1933) issue ($15.00) and the *first* brand new issue in 71 years, (#8, 2004, a trade paperback edition edited by Robert M. Price, $12.50).

#7: JANUARY 1933: This issue features Hugh B. Cave's classic "Murgunstrumm," as well as stories by Robert E. Howard, Henry S. Whitehead, and many more.

#8: Compiled by Robert M. Price, the former editor of *Crypt of Cthulhu* and numerous Lovecraftian anthologies, this issue offers the best in eldritch, scary, pulse-pounding entertainment. Featured in this issue are a great neo-pulp story by RICHARD LUPOFF; a Cthulhu Mythos story by Arkham House author GARY MYERS, continuing the adventures of Clark Ashton Smith's sorcerer Eibon in old Hyperborea; an eerie tale of the King in Yellow by STEFFAN B. ALETTI; a tale of cosmic horror and adventure by ADRIAN COLE, author of the VOIDAL series; one of DARRELL SCHWEITZER'S Sekenre tales, continuing the story of the hero of THE MASK OF THE SORCERER; and more!

CHOOSE FROM MORE GREAT WILDSIDE PRESS MAGAZINES!

Wildside Press is fast becoming the field's largest publisher of genre fiction magazines. Currently out or in production are no less than six fiction magazines: If you like *Strange Tales*, you might enjoy some of our other titles . . .

Adventure Tales . . . classic adventure tales from the pulps! #1 now available (featured author: Hugh B. Cave, plus many more classic pulp authors! $7.50); #2 coming in June (featured author: Nelson Bond). $19.95/4 issues.

Cat Tales . . . the firs all-cat fiction magazine! First issue currentl planned for Fall 2005. ($19.95/4 issues)

H.P. Lovecraft's Magazine of Horror . . . our flagship magazine, with many of the top names in horror, including Richard Matheson, Brian Lumley, Tanith Lee, etc. $7.50 for a sample issue, $19.95/4 issues.

Sherlock Holmes Mystery Magazine . . . edited by Marvin Kaye, SHMM debuts in November 2005!

Underworlds . . . the magazine of noir and suspense, now about to make its national debut! $19.95/4 issues.

Weird Tales . . . the grandfather of all horror magazines, presenting a classic mix of fantasy, horror, and the weird! Thomas Ligotti, Tanith Lee, Brian Lumley, Stephen King, Ramsey Campbell, David Schow, and many more have appeared in its pages over the years. Sample issue: $7.50. Subscription: $19.95/4 issues.

SPECIAL OFFER FOR *STRANGE TALES* READERS! Subscribe to any 4 magazines for $69.00 . . . save $10.80!

TO ORDER ONLINE: Visit www.wildsidepress.com.

1932) by Jack Williamson; "The Door to Saturn" (January, 1932), "The Second Interment" (January, 1933), "The Return of the Sorcerer" (September, 1931), "The Hunters from Beyond" (October, 1932), and "The Nameless Offspring" (June, 1932) by Clark Ashton Smith; "The Thing That Walked on the Wind" (January, 1933) and "The House in the Magnolias" (June, 1932) by August W. Derleth; "Cassius" (November, 1931) by Henry S. Whitehead; and "In the Lair of the Space Monsters" (October, 1932) by Frank Belknap Long. (Remember how, when Robert E. Howard decided to give the Conan tale "The Frost Giant's Daughter" to a fanzine, he changed the name of the hero to "Amra"? It was as if Conan was restricted to *Weird Tales*. In like manner, "People of the Dark" features a barbarian protagonist called Conan, but it's not the same one! It couldn't be, since the story was over in *Strange Tales*!) Other familar *Strange Tales* authors included Francis Flagg, Ray Cummings, and Arthur J. Burks.

It seems such a shame that the pulp folded so quickly.

And thus it seems incumbent upon a later generation of admirers to bring the old title back to life. *Weird Tales* has been revived more than once, and it is, fortunately, currently thriving. So why not bring back its competitor, or as I would rather regard it, its comrade and companion?

A crucial issue arises at just this point. What does it mean to revive *Strange Tales*? It means more than merely using the famous title again. For it would be a betrayal if a new *Strange Tales* lacked the proper continuity with the original run. There is absolutely no point in the bait and switch tactic of using the old title and hiding beneath it a handful of stories that one should never have expected to find in its pages. If the revived version is to possess authenticity, it will feature stories of more or less the same type, and by that I mean horror and fantasy stories of more or less classic type, with classic themes, though not hackneyed. Stories that ring new changes on the traditional themes. Tales with a sense of the pulps, though that description is inevitably vague. You will find no New Wave horror fiction here, no

WILDSIDE PRESS ORDER FORM

QUANTITY	TITLE	PRICE
	SUBTOTAL	
	In PA? Please add 6% State Sales Tax	
	U.S. Shipping & Handling: $3.95 for 1-2 books, $1 per additional book.	
	TOTAL	

Enclosed is payment of $_____ by ☐ check ☐ money order ☐ Visa ☐ MasterCard ☐ American Express.

NAME:_____

ADDRESS:_____

ADDRESS:_____

or order online at www.wildsidepress.com

CC# _____-_____-_____-_____

EXP: ____/____ Signature:_____

Mail to: Wildside Press LLC
P.O. Box 301
Holicong, PA 18928-0301

BY ROBERT M. PRICE

WILDSIDE PULP CLASSICS: PULP FACSIMILE SERIES

Series editor: John Gregory Betancourt

#1: *Spicy Mystery Stories* (August 1935)

Includes Robert Leslie Bellem, Atwater Culpepper, Ellery Watson Calder, Carl Moore, E. Hoffman Price, Arthur Wallace, and more.

#2: *Ghost Stories* (June 1931)

Stories by Conrad Richter (best known as the author of The Light in the Forest) and E. & H. Heron featuring psychic detective, Flaxman Low.

#3: *Spicy Mystery Stories* (February 1937)

The Feb. 1937 issue features Robert Leslie Bellem, Lew Merrill (Victor Rousseau) Hugh Speer, Justin Case (Hugh B. Cave), & many others!

#4: *Strange Tales #7* (January 1933)

This issue features Hugh B. Cave's classic "Murgunstrumm," as well as stories by Robert E. Howard, Henry S. Whitehead, and many more.

#5: *The Black Mask #2* (May 1920)

2nd issue of classic mystery mag, where hardboiled noir fiction was born!

#6: *Tales of Magic and Mystery* (February 1928)

Legendary rare early fantasy magazine!

#7: *The Phantom Detective #1* (February 1933)

The premiere issue of the detective-hero pulp!

#8: *Submarine Stories* (March 1930)

Rare pulp magazine, featuring stories and articles about (what else?) subs!

#9: *Sinister Stories #1* (Feb 1940)

The first issue of this "weird menace" pulp!

#10: *The Thrill Book* (Sept. 1, 1919)

The facsimile reprint from this legendary rare pulp magazine!

- -

Yes! Please send me the following books, for which I enclose payment. (Or order online with a credit card at www.wildsidepress.com, or through your favorite online bookseller.)

☐ *Spicy Mystery Stories* (Aug.1935) - $19.95
☐ *Ghost Stories* (June 1931) - $19.95
☐ *Spicy Mystery Stories* (Feb. 1937) - $19.95
☐ *Strange Tales #7* (January 1933) - $15.00
☐ *The Black Mask #2* (January 1920) - $19.95
☐ *Tales of Magic and Mystery* (Feb. 1928) - $19.95
☐ *The Phantom Detective #1* (Feb. 1933) - $19.95
☐ *Submarine Stories* (March. 1930) - $19.95
☐ *Sinister Stories* (Feb 1940) - $19.95
☐ *The Thrill Book* (Sept 1, 1919) - $19.95

Mail to: Wildside Press, P.O. Box 301
        Holicong, PA 18928-0301.
        www.wildsidepress.com

U.S. shipping: $3.95 for 1-2 books,
$1 per additional book. *Other countries:
please see www.wildsidepress.com*

Name: _____

Address: _____

Address: _____

Email: _____

surreal experiments. Please read no value judgment into this verdict: it just wouldn't be *Strange Tales*.

I daresay many of us remember *Strange Tales*, like *Weird Tales*, in large measure for being the initial vehicles of some major and minor Cthulhu Mythos stories by members of the Lovecraft Circle, for instance Clark Ashton Smith's only two stories featuring quotations from the *Necronomicon*. Readers first encountered Ithaqua, August Derleth's version of the Wendigo, in the pages of *Strange Tales*. The Cthulhu Mythos element can never be allowed to dominate the magazine, but it wouldn't be *Strange Tales* without it. We assure you, this publication will not be allowed to become one more haven for fan pastiches (though I will not criticize those guilty pleasures, either).

Personally, my favorite revival of *Weird Tales* was Lin Carter's four-book run for Zebra Books back in the 1980s, and that is high praise indeed, given the excellent quality of the issues produced by other hands since then. But I seek to emulate his approach of recapturing not only the actual likeness of the magazine but also the living legend of it, as seen through an intoxicating mist of nostalgia. I believe our first two Wildside Press issues of *Strange Tales* have met these goals admirably, and I will continue to strive to maintain those standards. I hope you will continue to support us as long as we deserve it.

This issue features the last story of the late, great Hugh B. Cave, "From the Pits of Elder Blasphemy," as well as an early and never-published tale by the legendary L. Sprague de Camp. Well-known weird poet Michael J. Fantina turns his talents to fiction in "The Return of the Spider Witch," while Charles Garofalo provides unwelcome glimpses of the fate awaiting any who do not like this issue! You may recognize Friday Jones as the editrix of the late, lamented magazine *Parts*. I believe all these (and our other) stories embody and convey the sense and feel of the pulps. We have made allowance for the somewhat different mores of the early twenty-first century, but we have sought never to snip the lines of continuity between our efforts and the wonderful fiction that inspired them. We hope you will agree. And of course you will read between the lines our submission guidelines! Ask yourself if that story you are thinking of submitting has the authentic pulp spirit. It's a bit intangible, as ghosts tend to be, but you'll be able to tell. And if not, we will. You may submit fiction and poetry to me by email at criticus@aol.com in MS Word or some IBM-compatible format.

We are fortunate to be able to feature the varied talents of Stanley Sargent who has both illustrated the issue and supplied the intriguing bits of strange lore inserted at intervals between the stories.

Strangely,

Robert M. Price
Hierophant of the Horde

THE LEGEND OF NITOCRIS

Some ancient sources mention King Menenre II and his sister-queen Nitocris as the successors to Pepi II, the fourth king of 6th Dynasty Egypt. The Egyptian priest Mantheo includes their names in his "official" but unreliable list of Egypt's rulers, describing Nitocris as "braver than all the men of her time, the most beautiful of all the women." Two hundred years earlier (c. 450 B.C.), the Greek historian Herodotus recorded the tale of the murder of an Egyptian king (probably Teti I, the first king of the 6th Dynasty) and the terrible retribution inflicted upon the perpetrators by the king's sister, widow and successor, Nitocris. Herodotus' story was recounted almost exactly in an early short story by Tennessee Williams, and authors H.P. Lovecraft, Brian Lumley, and others have since made Nitocris (a.k.a. Nitokris) an evil supernatural historical character.

No solid archaeological evidence exists to prove either Nitocris or her brother-husband-king actually existed, but inscriptions dating to the end of the 6th Dynasty are rare as the country was in total chaos due to its conquest by the Hyksos people from the Levant. Egyptologists prefer to classify the tale of Nitocris as legend until such time as physical evidence proves otherwise.

— Stanley C. Sargent

THE LEGEND OF NITOCRIS

RETURN OF THE SPIDER WITCH

by Michael J. Fantina

Dark magics pry this Spider's icy lid.
She rises in the Winter's frosty gale.
Her web is death, each grid on lethal grid,
Aslewzia, proud Sorceress of Bale.

A sterling evil, this dark arachnid,
Her suzerainty all lands bemoan, bewail.
Her arms and evils seeming myriad,
One royal child shall make her fall and fail.

— *Prophecy of Psil*

Snow, and the coming of snow, cold, and the coming of more cold, these were the prognostications, prophecies and rumors from the steppes. The great herds of woolly elephants, like armies of titan ghosts, moved through the undying snow to their secret places unmolested, though not unafraid. The season had come early, earlier than in living memory. It was hinted that the mythical sorceress, Aslewzia, had returned from her ice cave tomb where she had long been interred by heroes and wizards of eld, sealed with the Seven Abominable Signs of Umdrilkesh. Fear was in the land, in the snow, in the icy air, in the whispers of grand dames and grand sires, in the squealings of children and in the murmurings in the courts of kings. It was always the same: "Aslewzia the Eight-Armed, the Weaver of the Web of Death, the Spider Witch, the Long-Interred Sorceress, the Sorceress of Bale, is coming and will once again be among us to reestablish her Ice Throne of Topaz and Carnelian."

A thousand years gone Aslewzia had ruled the steppes, her minions and satraps lording it over all the lands of Ar as well as the numerous duchies between the mountains and the far salt sea. None knew her origins, only that one day she had appeared in the northern duchy of Broggolio. She had announced herself at the palace of the duke as a refugee queen. Her great beauty and charm won over all who saw her. However, that night, while seducing the duke in his private chambers she apparently devoured him, leaving nothing. The following morning she declared herself the rightful Duchess of Broggolio. The relatives and palace guard failed to see the humor of her declaration and assaulted her in a body. The Spider Witch revealed her true form and very few, indeed, left the palace grounds alive. Her will became the law of the duchy. Myth related that

she seduced, devoured and then ruled several nearby dukes in a similar manner.

Eventually she raised armies among these duchies and led them very successfully into battle. Indeed, many opposing armies fled the field when they perceived a giant spider with a human head leading its human troops into battle.

The Sorceress of Bale had raised a great throne for herself hewn of crystal and inlaid with huge stones of topaz and carnelian. At the base of Mount Ki, at the foot of the glacier, she caused to be raised a great city and a palace wherein she placed the throne of topaz and carnelian and ruled therefrom. Here it was, exactly ten centuries ago, that a rebel band of warriors and wizards assaulted Aslewzia at the pinnacle of her pride and power. They were armed with potent and arcane magics rarely seen in that day, among these were the Seven Abominable Signs of Umdrilkesh, this being a series of spells to seal any evil for one thousand years. The assault on the Spider Witch had proven successful. She had been caught asleep and a quarterstaff of enchanted hornbeam had been driven through her black heart. An ensorcelled sarcophagus of ice was prepared, and she was interred in her own palace. Her minions fled and the peoples were freed. The encroaching glacier eventually claimed her palace and city in the ensuing centuries.

Now the spell was up.

Trothule, the hoary monarch of Ar, the Land of the Two Rivers, sat his throne, uneasy. The dome of the great hall rose in polished arcs of ivory. The floor was heavy timber highly polished and curiously inlaid with lapis lazuli and river pearls. Two great fires glowed from their stone hearths within the hall, its walls hung with the wooly skins of elephants. The great lord and the members of his court were robed and clothed with bear skins, ermine and multi-hued wool.

Jayz, the green-eyed, crimson-haired and pearly pale daughter of King Trothule, sat near her father, and she was a wonder to behold: lovely as a goddess, swift as an arrow and as graceful as a bird. Though barely nineteen, she sat in the councils of the king's court, as she had since a small child, at her own insistence — for her father could deny her nothing — and offered advice while listening carefully to the counsel of others. She, as her father, had always held the protection of Ar and its great city as their foremost goal. Through war and peace, and especially during the last few years, her counsel had proven to be a marvel to all, even to her father.

Rogg, the Neckbreaker, fourth cousin to Jayz, was an ardent suitor of the princess. A dull-witted but brave lad, he spoke from his seat near a brazier where he warmed his huge hands.

"My great king, and Jayz, the very light of the world, I tell you, fear is a thing unknown to me!"

As Rogg spoke, Jayz, who was in animated though quiet consultation with a valued counselor nearby, interrupted her dialogue to whisper: "Fear, my dear Rogg, is only one of the many things unknown to thee!"

The huge warrior, even if he had heard Jayz, which was doubtful, might have guessed her words a poetic compliment that was beyond him. He continued with a litany of warriors, dragons, wizards and assorted monsters that he had dispatched during the past dozen or so years. The eyes of all there assembled glazed over. While his great courage and strength were never in doubt, his approach to a problem was complete bafflement if he could not kill something.

A dozen or so female servants stepped lightly into the great hall with trenchers full of steaming mugs of wine and beer. The king and his princess were served first. Then the remaining nobles and their hangers-on took each a flagon.

It was early evening, overcast and snowing heavily. The wind, howling like some immense bird of prey, seemed to cast a spell of nameless dread over those gathered there. They all fell silent, brooding, save for a few whispered words among the servants. The evening was oppressive.

Cargelo, the court wizard, a beloved, elderly man known more for affability and good counsel than his prowess with spells and conjurations, arose slowly from his short ivory chair and moved toward one of the many braziers which smoldered in the center of the great hall near King Trothule's throne. He extended his cold hands to warm himself as many others had been doing all day. Suddenly there was a sound like the timbers of a great ship groaning in her death agonies. It reverberated from ceiling to floor, and all gaped in amazement. The brazier in front of Cargelo flared up, and the long glowing tongues of flame shot up greenly, twisting themselves into the image of a man.

All took a step back and gasped. Rogg drew his huge sword but was stayed by a wave from Jayz's hand. The verdant flames assembled themselves into the discernable form of the long dead wizard Grotherian. "Beware," he spoke, in a voice like rolling thunder. "Beware!"

Cargelo, nearest the apparition, replied: "Ah, first wizard of Ar, Founder of our City, dead these countless millennia, what brings you to the land of the living? What danger do you herald?"

"Beware, my portent is of doom, doom!" repeated the imperious form of the sorcerer as he floated a foot above the burning embers of the brazier. "Beware the Spider Witch, she who has come forth from the tomb to reclaim the Topaz Throne. She means to lay waste the City of Ar and all her lands, enslave her peoples and slay all the royal family!"

"And how, pray tell," expostulated Cargelo, "does Aslewzia plan to accomplish her mission?"

There was a long pause; then the ghost spoke again. "Through subterfuge, seduction and death…behold!"

Here Grotherian, who, in life, had been the most powerful wizard in the history of Ar, raised his arms as if to make ready to fly. The scene in the great hall changed. Suddenly the royal group, servants and all found themselves in a gigantic cavern of ice. "Fear not, my uninitiated brethren, this is not real but merely the vision-of-what-is-real."

In one corner of the cavern, a scarce few feet from where Jayz stood, was a sarcophagus of ice. Slowly the nude, noble form of a tall woman sat up within the coffin and, most nimbly, stepped out. She was indeed tall, of uncertain age somewhere between eighteen and forty, and ineffably beautiful in an unearthly, almost eerie fashion. Her hair was long and black, like silk. Her skin was a rich deep, deep tan, her eyes dead black like polished jet. She was tall, tall above the normal, her body sculpted like some idol. She strode, as one long accustomed to the wielding of authority, to a teak-paneled wardrobe.

The king's court stared in bizarre fascination like unaccustomed voyeurs. While they could see, they could not hear anything in this conjured vision. They knew however, beyond any doubt, that they were seeing images of the dread Spider Witch, the sometimes Eight-Armed Aslewzia.

They gaped as Aslewzia stood with her back to them before her wardrobe. Suddenly her body went into contortions impossible for any human being. Like children caught in some terrible nightmare, they watched in horror as, one after another, six new arms erupted from her back and sides, three on each side, right down to her waist, complete with shoulder blades.

She was still now, but for the opening of her extra arms, stretching like a dreamer awakened from a long sleep.

The Spider Witch opened the wardrobe to reveal a very large mirror. She stood before this screen, admiring herself. The gazers could see the terrible pride she took in the image of herself, her beautiful, terrible smile as she ran her many hands over her body: stomach, thighs, breasts, hair and buttocks.

Then, once again, they watched in renewed horror as her body went into contortions once more and bent itself over double and her awful, impossible arms began to change into legs. While her arms had appeared human, these new legs left all womanish semblance behind. Even her two natural legs underwent a metamorphosis. These were sleek powerful, many-jointed limbs, bearing razorlike projections on the lower joints, which ended in unique hoofs that seemed hard as steel. Her breasts hung hugely, pendulously, under her torso, while her face, head and hair remained exactly the same. Even the expression on her face was unchanged, her smile irresistible, deadly.

As the rapt and terrified audience gazed on this eight-armed, now eight-legged creature, she turned her terrible head directly toward Jayz and seemed actually to recognize that her privacy had been invaded. Aslewzia's lips curled wickedly, she spoke in a voice like a sheering avalanche: "Jayz, Princess of Ar, last of your line, you shall die by my machinations. . . ."

Once again with a sound like great groaning timbers Aslewzia and her cavern disappeared, and the royal entourage found themselves once more in the great hall. Grotherian's unstable form still hovered over the brazier. "Powerful, powerful is she! Even more than any had guessed. She has discovered and broken my splendid and twice potent spell...."

"Master," pleaded Cargelo, "what are we to do? How do we defend ourselves against..."

He was interrupted by plaintive ghostly tones: "Look to the *Blood Book of Psil*, page 771. . . . "

With this admonition the ghost of Grotherian disappeared in a gaudy display of sparks.

The old king shouted orders and cleared the great hall of all but his most trusted warriors and advisors, then called for the *Blood Book of Psil* to be brought to him. Within minutes Trothule, Jayz, Rogg, Cargelo and a few other trusted souls sat around the great oak table as Cargelo thumbed the magical tome known as the *Blood Book of Psil*. Hastily he moved to page 771, in the section called "Prophecies Major Minor Outré and Jejune."

He ran his bony, gnarled index finger down the large vellum page filled with strange half-cuneiform, half-hieroglyphic symbols written in an ancient effete, long-dead hand.

Rogg, Jayz, and the king pressed close to the old sorcerer as he mumbled to himself. "Ah, ha!" he expostulated at last, "Here it is, prophetic poem 7,641, under the subsection 'Outré Prophecies.'"

The graceful Jayz, with little discernable effort, directed the hulking Rogg and the bony little sorcerer out of her way, saying kindly, "Excuse me gentlemen, may I? I am able to read this text with an even more acute and precise pronunciation than the worthy Cargelo."

Her petite index finger, with the prettily lacquered red nail showing a miniature painting of the first queen of Ar, moved to the designated passage. She read, evenly and distinctly, in a wonderful sing song voice:

> Dark magics pry this Spider's icy lid.
> She rises in the Winter's frosty gale.
> Her web is death, each grid on lethal grid,
> Aslewzia, proud Sorceress of Bale.
>
> A sterling evil, this dark arachnid,
> Her suzerainty all lands bemoan, bewail,
> Her arms and evils seeming myriad,
> One royal child shall make her fall and fail.

As she spoke, or more accurately, sang these verses, the small group was conscious of a strange preternatural force amongst them. They felt somehow electrified, transported

by a potency of immense magical realms. It filled them all briefly, and then was gone.

"By the Seven Signs! By the immortal Slid herself!" shouted Cargelo. "'Tis is a potent rune, meant to be sung by an especial one and by him only unto the devastation of Aslewzia! My king, your daughter, the lovely and elfin Jayz, is the sorceress who will crush the Spider Witch like a frozen cockroach on an iron anvil!"

"I am no sorceress," spoke the princess quietly but sternly. "I have always eschewed the dark arts."

"Ah, that is only too well known to me, my bird-like royal one, however, your intonation of these phrases has proven you to be a powerful sorceress, though unschooled. Indeed, I have read this passage many times through the years, as indeed I have read and reread the *Blood Book of Psil* many times over, but when *you* read that passage the power of sorcery is in it! This passage sung in the presence of the eight-armed Spider Witch will lay her low for a thousand years. It is given only to one in a millennium to be ordained to such a task. You are the only living bane of her who seeks to regain the Ice Throne of Topaz and Carnelian."

All gaped at Jayz as they heard the words of old Cargelo. "Then she is overthrown?" asked the princess, quizzically.

"Ah, no, no, my pretty one," continued the old sorcerer. "These eight lines must be spoken, sung, within very *close proximity* to that evil arachnid to have the desired effect. You must, my precious royal one, make haste for the glacier and descend to the ice palace in the lost city of Aslewiza to bind her once again with this spell."

Jayz grabbed the grizzled old mage by the shoulders and looked squarely in his rheumy eyes with her magically green gaze. "Cargelo, how certain are you of this? It seems a rash statement on its face. We have the deepest love and respect for you, but are you *certain?*"

The old mage let out a long, sad sigh. "Oh, splendid one, gladly would I go in your stead. And, indeed, I will go if you and the king but say the word, though my magics be feeble and largely ineffective as you only too well know. I will certainly do my best. Gladly would I die for you and this kingdom, princess, but it would be to no avail."

There were tears in his eyes as he finished speaking, for all who knew him knew well he spoke truth. He was a stout heart.

"Nonsense," cried Trothule, "my daughter to seek out the Spider herself? Never! I will see myself dead first."

"Aye, to that!" shouted the bombastic Rogg. He drew his huge falchion, covered with runes naming the monsters that had died by its wielding. "All I am certain of is that I will protect the delicate flower known as Jayz with my life and sword! I will slay the monster myself in her icy lair as she stands, sits or squats upon her Ice Throne of Topaz and Carnelian! I will cleave the fell head from her leggy body and gouge out the topaz and carnelian jewels to bring a fine present for Jayz."

But even as they levied their protests, both the king and the Neckbreaker, though somewhat lacking in the gift of perception, clearly understood that old Cargelo would never have ventured such a suggestion had there been the slightest possibility of some other course of action.

"So be it!" Jayz whispered just audibly enough for all there present to hear. "But first, magician, clarify for me precisely how I shall incant these eight lines of magic, this potent spell as you say? Must I be outside? In daylight, full moon? Must it be sung in a certain key? Whispered in Aslewzia's ear? Her left ear? Her right? Must she be sleeping? Must I be in her embrace, and is she to coax and prompt me as she devours me?"

There was a sly, though not cruel, smile on the girl's face as she interrogated old Cargelo.

"Close," he whispered, "close, though I know not how close." He sighed again and continued. "Sung or spoken, it will work its magic equally well, Princess, day or night, full moon or no."

"Father, I leave in the morning with Rogg, the Neckbreaker. The two of us will make the seventeen league trip to the glacier and there find or effect an opening in the ice, descend to the Cavern of the Spider and there, it is to be hoped, dispatch her with a song…. no, sweet father, you cannot, dare not dissuade me. I have made my decision."

The snow was deep as they left the palace and the great city of Ar. The two of them on horseback left without servants, accompanied by a single mule with food, a tent and extra weapons which the Neckbreaker had insisted upon taking along.

Shortly it began to snow again as the pair wound their way northwards, along the old tortuous pike road that led to the mountains and the great glacier and lost city of the Eight-Armed Sorceress.

The wind rose up. They tightened their great robes of shaggy elephant hide about them, and their progress was slow, tedious.

They saw no one and, though it was still early, the landscape had the aspect of dreadful night, a preternatural permanent twilight as though the sun might never again win free. Evil was abroad.

After several hours they stopped at a place where Rogg's keen senses told him there was the cottage of a millwright distantly related to him, a place he had stopped ofttimes in the past for hot food or a cool drink.

From the snow-paved road they could see nothing, but Rogg made a way through the snowdrifts and after a few minutes they found a huge hump of snow with a small chimney, white smoke pumping from it.

They dismounted, the Neckbreaker making a fuss about lifting Jayz from her mount. Rogg's huge hand swept snow away from the upper door and he pounded vigorously, shouting, "Open, damn you!"

"By the great Slid," came a response from within. "It is the Spider Witch come to eat me! Ah, wretch, I will sell myself dearly! You'll see!" With these words the door opened inward to reveal a short, bearded man brandishing a large fork.

"Keltus!" shouted Jayz's suitor, "would you do in your kith and kin with the tines of a fork? An ignominious end to the great Rogg!"

"Rogg!" shouted the little man, a great smile spreading across his face as he embraced the warrior. "It is a blessing to see such a welcome relative. I thought I might not live to see another human face. And who, pray tell is this?" he said as he put down the fork and ushered them both into his warm home. "Some sweet tart from the brothels of Drumchee? And so lovely she is, fit to be a princess I dare say! A sight more comely than that old shrew of a princess Jayz, eh?"

Rogg's face froze and crimsoned. He could barely speak, though he managed to say, "No!"

"Ah, then from the brothels of Castelius, for a certainty! Ah, she is a rare beauty, I can easily see!"

At this point the princess was removing her heavy coat and head ware, and her brilliant crimson hair fell in great tides down her shoulders.

"Rogg," continued his relative, "yes, it is from the Brothels of Castelius, after all! I see you have spared no expense this time, my friend, but opened your tight purse wide…"

Jayz smiled broadly at the monumental embarrassment of Rogg just as the Neckbreaker shouted at the top of his lungs: "Idiot! This is the Princess Jayz of Ar, daughter of our great liege lord King Trothule! On your knees! I shall lop off your worthless head!"

All three of them began to shout at this point. The little bearded millwright tangled with Rogg at close quarters, swearing loudly and but half-aware of what the Neckbreaker was saying and shouting.

The princess, in no mood for this, shouted at the top of her lungs for the pair to desist. Twenty minutes later found a sullen and mumbling Rogg sipping mulled wine with the princess, on the opposite side of the small table, drinking a spiced and steaming clay mug of beer.

Keltus returned to the table with two trenchers of sausage and black bread and seated himself between the two royals. The mumbling Rogg was heard to say something about peasants kneeling before royalty, but Jayz quickly shushed him.

If Keltus felt any special embarrassment at his insulting comments about the princess he made no allusion to it, but quickly and succinctly answered all of Jayz's questions. She learned that they were about two days' ride, because of the snow, away from the glacier and the frozen city of Aslewzia.

The helpful and energetic millwright offered to lead them there himself. Though the Neckbreaker protested, Jayz happily agreed.

Dawn of the third day of travel found the princess, the warrior and the millwright standing on the windswept glacier. Each was heavily wrapped in wool garments and thick, furry animal hides against the extreme cold. Their mounts had been hidden behind a snowdrift where a stand of evergreens gave them some protection.

The little millwright looked up into the green eyes of his princess. "Ah, my princess, I have led you here, but now I have not even the vaguest notion of where to look for the damned queen or her infernal city!"

The three figures huddled close together, saying nothing as each pondered their next step. They had not long to wait as suddenly the screaming winds died down and an odd, though familiar greenish image appeared before them. It was the not unwelcome spirit of the Great Grotherian himself!

"By the goddess Slid herself!" stammered the millwright, "This time it is the evil Spider Witch come to eat us all!"

"Silence, you idiot," Rogg intoned through gritted teeth.

Jayz bade the moribund sorcerer to speak. Grotherian skipped all portentous announcements of his advent and simply instructed the trio to walk, three abreast, for exactly one hundred paces. Then the entrance to the palace of Aslewzia should be revealed to them. The shade disappeared in a burst of sparks.

The three trudged off doggedly as the snow and screaming winds resumed and, carefully counting, they reached step ninety-nine. Then, each raising his right foot high into the air, they brought them down with a pronounced degree of force. *Crash!* The ice beneath them shattered and caved in. They fell precipitously down a long chute of ice and snow for several minutes. The only sounds they heard were the screams of the millwright, Keltus, and the cursing of Rogg, each measuring by his profanities his rapid accumulation of bruises and bumps.

In the end they were deposited unceremoniously into a thickly carpeted chamber of stone, with paneled walls of distantly imported teak inlaid with silver, mother-of-pearl and aquamarine. The room smelled of stale musk and great age.

"I like not this place!" So spoke the princess as she helped the millwright and the Neckbreaker up from the floor — they had landed a good deal harder than had she. "I can feel the trace of an evil sorcery in the air. Certainly we are close to the Spider Witch's own lair."

Rogg drew his great sword, the millwright his notched and double-headed axe, and the princess kept her hand on the pommel of her long dirk. The trio filed slowly and carefully out the single door of the room, which was slightly ajar.

The chamber door opened into a huge hall of purple stone with long slit windows through which no light penetrated as the palace was encased within the living glacier. A weird preternatural luminescence radiated from iridescent gems within the purple masonry. At various places along these walls were plaster frescos amazing and bizarre, scenes out of a madman's nightmare. Giant spiders of every form and description were depicted in these scenes, performing abominable acts scarcely mentionable or even recognizable.

They filed past these odd artistries full of astonishment and wonder, and, indeed, fear. At length they came upon the entrance to a long, high corridor paneled in rosewood and ebony, and inlaid with fine silver threads so that the effect was as one walking down a long tunnel of webs woven by a giant spider.

The air was chilly, close, scented with a sickly sweet, mildly intoxicating aroma. At the far end of the corridor was an iron-hasped door of heavy ebony and upon it was a plaque of brass. In three hieroglyphic languages were written the Seven Abominable Signs of Umdrilkesh.

The companions stood before this portal. "Behold! Can you read it princess?" interrogated the smaller man.

"Indeed, millwright, it is the spell which has bound the spider sorceress these many centuries, though now its potency has reached its end. Within a few more days, according to our beloved Cargelo, Aslewzia will have recovered her complete powers and any opportunity we may have had of dispatching her will be extremely slim indeed."

The Neckbreaker drew his sword. "I say we stove in the door, rush her, and dice her into a spider succotash, before she has the chance to grow the arms and legs!"

"Not wise, I counsel, my dear Rogg," whispered the princess. "The door, as you may perceive, is solid ebony imported from beyond the Southern Sea. It would take hours for even you to hack through it. And the ensuing racket would certainly alert our many-legged, multi-armed nemesis."

At this point the teeth of the little millwright began to chatter, and he spoke haltingly. "Perhaps I should return to the chamber from whence we came and, um, act as a rear guard? So that we might make good our escape if all else fails?"

"Coward!" spoke Rogg from between his gritted teeth, and there was murder in his eyes.

Jayz put a hand on the arm of the Neckbreaker. "Enough! Remember, he volunteered to bring us here, or we would have spent forever on these accursed ice fields on a fool's errand. And he is not a warrior by trade."

Rogg seemed somewhat placated, though he had been sullen since the brief melee in the cottage of his relative. "My sweet little bird, Jayz, I'm at my wits' end. I know not

how to proceed. If I cannot swing my blade…"

An unaccustomed look descended upon the face of the pretty princess. It was a look of resignation, purpose, full of an athletic energy akin to sadness. She took hold of the collars of both the frightened Keltus and the bemused Rogg and tightly yanked on them.

"Listen, and listen carefully, for the time is near, I feel it. You must give me the chance to speak the magic poem-rune, which will re-entomb the Spider Witch. That alone must be your task. The king and indeed all the peoples of Ar depend upon you two!"

The millwright took a deep breath to still his fear, and Rogg let out a sigh releasing his weight of helplessness. He was about to ask how they might enter the sealed chamber when the princess, letting go the two, turned gracefully toward the ebony door, grasped the iron handle, and pulled. Despite, or rather perhaps because of its weight, the door opened readily. It was not locked.

The door swung outward without a sound as though its hinges had been oiled every week for the past ten centuries. They stepped quietly into the room. It was easy to see that this was the very chamber magically shown to them by the wizard Grotherian in the king's hall. Ahead of them, with her back to the trio, stood a tall, willowy woman with a dark green robe, silver of trim, wrapped tightly about her. Without turning, Aslewzia spoke. "Ah, I have been expecting this intrusion for some time. So glad you could make it and see the Sorceress of Bale, eternal queen of Ar, with your own eyes. And, too, I have grown hungry with my long, long sleep, and I only dine on royal flesh."

So saying, Aslewzia threw off her green robe, revealing herself in all her naked and hideous beauty. She turned, her eight arms waving eerily, dressed only in a tiny silver chatelaine and platform boots.

With a loud warrior's cry the Neckbreaker was nearly upon her before she deftly side-stepped him, moved to a rack of weapons and simultaneously withdrew no fewer than eight gleaming swords. She hefted them expertly.

Rogg turned and drew a second sword with his free hand from the arsenal he carried with him. "Prepare to die, spider!"

The two of them flew at each other and then fell quickly apart. Rogg had received only three cuts by some miracle, while the Spider Witch was yet unscathed. Suddenly, as if sensing real and unexpected danger, she turned from him and fell upon Jayz. The princess saw her coming and quickly raised a heavy oak chair to protect herself. Four swords wielded by four different arms battered the chair. Jayz was knocked across the room and into the far wall where she found herself mired in the sticky strands of a great cobweb. She was only half-conscious as her head had struck the stone beneath the webs. She was trapped, spread-eagled in an upright position against the wall, held fast by the adamantine web.

Now the two men fell to the attack. The millwright was not unschooled in the art of axe-wielding and, with the help of Rogg's two swords, he lasted for nearly three seconds until he was felled by a well-aimed blow from Aslewzia's second left arm. The sword parted his helmet like an ax through a rotten board. Then by a small miracle Rogg, on a swift and unexpected uppercut, hacked off her right, bottom-most arm just above the wrist. Wincing, the Spider Witch never seemed to miss a beat or a thrust with her remaining seven arms. The Neckbreaker felt a ray of hope at this piece of good luck, but it was short-lived. The injured arm of Aslewzia sprayed black blood for several seconds as she continued the fight. But then the blood stopped and, much to his horror, the missing hand grew back in seconds, emerging from the stump as an ordinary human hand might through the mouth of an empty sleeve! Deftly it retrieved the sword from its fallen predecessor.

The spider beat back Rogg, inexorably, with her tremendous advantage. Perhaps no other warrior then living could have lasted as long he, but the end was inevitable. She backed him to her ice coffin where she had lain for a thousand years with a hornbeam staff stuck through her black heart. At length six of her arms, the upper three on each side, parried his two swords to the outside, while her two bottom-most arms ran him through. He fell back into her sarcophagus.

Her spider face was flushed with her victory, purpling more deeply around her cluster of faceted eyes. She carefully cleaned the blood from off each of her eight swords and dropped them back into their rack. Then, as if she suddenly remembered some urgency or felt something unexpected, she turned swiftly to the far wall where the princess was pinioned, groaning.

"I smell the stench of a potent sorcery not my own!" she hissed. She bent over double, and her arms and legs underwent the metamorphosis. Within seconds she was on six spider legs, keeping her two uppermost arms as they were. Folding these she scampered to the princess.

Aslewzia eyed the princess, running her hands through Jayz's hair and over her body, like some bizarre craftsman carefully looking for flaws in his prized piece. The arachnid queen sensed the throbbing of unknown magic. Her preternaturally intuitive mind sought some solution to this riddle. The princess was no sorceress. Or *was* she? There was something about her, her presence. Certainly, Aslewzia knew, Jayz had never studied the arcane arts; she was too young. But still there was something strange, something that hinted of immense and untapped powers. She shivered. No matter, she thought. In minutes she would devour the princess, leave the confines of her iced-in tomb, gain allies and bend them to her will, re-establish her satraps throughout the land and rule in splendor as of old.

The unconscious princess groaned and opened her green eyes. The black nightmare eyes of the Spider Witch greeted her. Aslewzia smiled broadly. "There, there, pretty little princess you've hurt yourself. But fear not, soon you will be beyond pain as these other two idiots are."

Jayz stared back, eyes aglow with power, at the spider. Then Aslewzia was seized with a half-formed, unnamed revelation. Here was danger, in an unknown form.

The princess moved her lips, "Dark magics pry this Spider's icy lid, She rises in the Winter's frosty gale. . . ."

Immediately, the left hand of the Spider Witch was at the throat of the princess, cutting off air and sound. She knew, instinctively, that there was danger in these words. Why or how, though, she was uncertain. For the first time the Spideress began to learn fear. Was it even possible that a mere human, a girl, though royal, unschooled in the arcana of sorcery, could possess such magic? She bristled at the thought. And yet she felt within the small body a thrice-potent power that could be lethal to her and her fell plans of domination. Fascination mingled with fear. She wanted to crush the throat of the princess but was half spellbound by the mystery of what manner of entity this Jayz might be.

Too late, Aslewzia sensed another danger. There was a loud yell as she felt the Neckbreaker, bleeding profusely, jump upon her back and ram the forgotten hornbeam staff, which he retrieved from the sarcophagus where he had fallen, through her spider thorax, piercing the black heart.

She released Jayz and with two of her spider legs flicked off Rogg as though he were of no weight. She screamed loudly, inhumanly, as she reached back with her two human arms and grabbed the hornbeam staff. Black blood was coursing and spouting everywhere. Try as she might, she could not pull the magical spear free. She scampered about the room, overturning heavy furniture in her struggles. Then, on the far side of the chamber, when it appeared that she might actually yank the stick from her heart, the Spider Witch heard a beautiful sing-song voice.

> *Dark magics pry this Spider's icy lid.*
> *She rises in the Winter's frosty gale.*
> *Her web is death, each grid on lethal grid,*
> *Aslewzia, proud Sorceress of Bale.*
>
> *A sterling evil, this dark arachnid,*
> *Her suzerainty all lands bemoan, bewail.*
> *Her arms and evils seeming myriad,*
> *One royal child shall make her fall and fail.*

Aslewzia began to scream terribly, horribly as her life's blood coursed faster and faster from her hideous body. Still she tugged at the hornbeam staff. Now she began to slow in her actions: her head fell forward, her hands released the staff. Her awful legs began to curl up under her and she fell heavily upon the stone floor.

Jayz watched all of this, still pinioned to the wall in the spider's web. Her head ached terribly, but her thoughts were of both Rogg and the millwright.

The princess lost consciousness. The next thing she remembered, she was again in the hut of the millwright. But this time she was in his bed, Rogg and his kinsman standing over her, looking nervously at her. They were each something to behold. The millwright's head was bound up in heavy bandages, his right eye covered. Rogg was bare-chested but bound in heavy white linen covering his stab wounds.

"By Slid herself!" shouted the Neckbreaker triumphantly. "She lives, and now we can be married!"

The soft clear voice of the princess was heard to say, "I hope you will be very happy with him, millwright."

Michael Fantina has had scores of poems published in the USA, Canada, and Great Britain. Some of these have appeared in The Lyric, Candelabrum, Romantics Quarterly, The New Formalist, Contemporary Poetry, The Sonnet Scroll, The Book of Eibon, *and* Lost Worlds of Space and Time. *He has worked at Florida International University and at Rutgers University.*

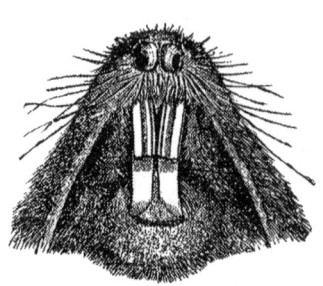

JADED

by Ann K. Schwader

I long to learn of wisdom found
Through mildewed tomes locked underground
In wizards' lairs & ghouls' retreats,
The haunts of Si'lats & ifrits.
I crave that esoteric lore
Which blotted stars out long before
R'lyeh withdrew beneath the sea
To threaten dreamers' sanity.
I have a passion to peruse
The inspirations of that Muse
Who whispered low in Geoffrey's ears
& spurred young Edward Derby's fears.
Away with texts mundane & tame!
I thirst to know each nameless Name,
The hieroglyphs of Irem's tombs,
The lost details of Sarnath's doom,
The moon-rites of the restless dead . . .
I want to read what Alhazred.

CAPTAIN LEOPARD

by L. Sprague de Camp

[This tale is based upon a lost work by the second-century Platonic philosopher Kelsos or Celsus, who wrote a treatise called *A True Word*, attacking Christianity and presenting the story of Panthera and Miriam. We know most of the content of Celsus' work because the Church father Origenes wrote a verbose attack on it, *Against Celsus*, which survives.]

Herondas waved me to the new table and chairs in his *potisterion*, behind the counter. "After all," he said, "you talked me into installing them. Whether they are worth the extra rent I have to pay for the space remains to be seen. Space in Damascus is hellishly costly."

I had scarcely sat down when this burly, gray-haired centurion in full Roman legionary accouterments appeared. I knew he was a centurion by the transverse crest on his helmet.

Herondas instantly became the cringing courtier: "Oh, Captain! I have just the place for you!" He waved to the other chair at my little table. "I have some delicious Falernian...."

When the centurion made for the vacant chair, I rose, expecting him to want the table to himself. But he carefully laid his helmet on the table and said: "No, no, sit down, my good man! There's no sense in having one of those fine chairs go to waste." Then to Herondas: "A *sextarius* of that Falernian, please."

The accent of his Latin said: "Greek Alexandria!" as plainly as if it had been painted on his forehead. Since his manners were better than one expects of an officer in an army of occupation, I said:

"*Hellenizeis?*"

"Oh, good! You speak Greek," he replied in that tongue.

"So there are at least two civilized men in Damascus. I am Gaius Julius Panthera, *posterior hostatus* of the third cohort of the Legion Six Ferrata. In the original Greek it was *Pardalis*, meaning that big spotted cat they fetch from Africa for shows in the arena. But the Romans translated it when I enlisted. And you, my good sir?"

"Nobody; just Claudius Dion, factor for Maesius the importer. In Latin they bobtail my name to Dio. Pleased to meet you, Captain Leopard."

By now the centurion had drunk a large goblet of Herondas' Falernian, enough to affect one's balance. But the centurion, being an old soldier, showed no effects. He signaled for a second, indicating one for me as well. While waiting, he said:

"Friend Dion, you may be just the man I am looking for. You see, my twenty years are up in a few days, so I am looking for a safe place to invest my *praemia militiae*." He meant his discharge bonus.

"You are not staying on, then?"

The centurion tossed back his head. "*Ouden ge!* There's a rumor that the Ironclad Sixth is to be shifted back to Judaea, and I saw all I want of that country when we were posted there thirty years ago...."

For a while we talked of Maesius' business, with its far-flung import accounts and its profits and losses. Somehow Panthera's service in Judaea came up again. He said:

"Besides, going back there might subject me to certain — ah — domestic embarrassments."

"Indeed?"

"Yes, sir! You see, I formed an attachment there to a Jewish girl. She'd be an aging woman now, of course, but my present mate is looking forward to a proper wedding as soon as I'm paid off. She would take umbrage if my long-ago light-o'-love came back into our lives. My mate of many years is a fiery Galatian Celt. Are you married, Dion?"

"Yes. Three children, plus one that died of a sickness."

"Then you know what I mean."

"Sure. Who was this onetime light-o'-love?"

"Just a pretty little Jewish girl named Miriam, the betrothed of a carpenter named Joseph. During our love affair, she became pregnant. When her state became obvious, the carpenter dumped her. The Jews have an official procedure for breaking a betrothal, like a divorce, and the carpenter took advantage of it."

"What happened then?"

"She took her infant, our baby son, to Egypt looking for work. This child she named Yeshua, a good Jewish name, which becomes *Iesous* in Greek and *Jesus* in Latin, since those languages have no *sh* sound.

"Anyway, I understand, this kid grew up in Egypt. Miriam managed to get him an education of sorts on her slim housekeeper's pay at the Jewish temple. He also studied at the Egyptian temple, where they worship gods with the heads of lions, hippopotami, and other beasties. The priests who tutored the lad, finding him a promising youth, taught him some of the tricks they use to beguile their faithful into thinking they can do real magic and miracles.

"In time, Miriam and Yeshua came back to Judaea. To

make a living, Yeshua showed off some of his Egyptian tricks and soon had a following who would swear he could work genuine miracles.

"So, they reasoned, he must be some sort of demigod, with a divine father. Since his followers were mostly Jews, they got the idea that this divine parent must be Yahveh, the bad-tempered, bloodthirsty Judaean chief god. I've heard that, when they asked Yeshua about it, he gave evasive answers.

"Eventually all this talk of a half-divine son of Yahveh came to the ears of the Sanhedrin, a council of Jewish priests who had jurisdiction in some criminal and civil cases. Since a main tenet of Judaism is that Yahveh is the one and only real god in existence, you can see why they would not put up with this demigod fable.

"Of course, in the Mediterranean world we are used to demigods. Asklepios, the founder of medicine, they say was the child of Apollo and the mortal maid Koronis — unless this Koronis got herself pregnant the same way my Miriam did and then blamed it on the first god who came to mind. After all, if your daughter tells you she lost her virginity to a god, you don't dare punish her severely. She just might be telling the truth, in which case the god in question might resent your chastisement of one of his light loves.

"But the Jews are funny that way. Nowadays most educated people know that men make gods in their own image. As Xenophanes said, if horses had gods, those gods would have manes and hooves. So we civilized folk don't take theological disputes seriously.

"But things are different in this part of the world. Many Jews take their theology very seriously indeed, especially those who call themselves Pharisees. I wish we had more of them in the Sixth. They are fierce fighters and, I think, more trustworthy than the general run of folk. If you give one an order, in plain, definite language, he'll carry it out or die trying.

"But the Jews have persuaded the Emperors to excuse them from military duty. The reason they give is that they would have to swear Roman oaths, which they consider against their religion."

"What became of Yeshua?"

"It's a sad story. The Sanhedrin persuaded the Procurator, Pontius Pilatus, to arrest Yeshua so they could try him for heresy. This is a serious matter to the Jews, and one convicted thereof is deemed worthy of death.

"Pilatus was a strict disciplinarian who went by the letter of the law, and a strong believer in doing things the old Roman way. He had caused disturbances before — something about bringing army standards, with their little statues on poles, into Jerusalem. Some Jews thought that an outrage, violating their ancient prohibition of works of art. When there were riots, with people sworded to death, Rome sent Pilatus a warning to be more careful of these people's religious sensitivities.

"So his soldiers rounded up young Yeshua, who had been promoting some kind of reformed Judaism, with doctrines of extreme altruism. If someone assaulted you to rob you, he preached, you shouldn't resist but let him have his way. To any manly Greek — or Roman, either — that would seem crazy advice; but that's what they say he said.

"After a hearing, Pilatus said he did not think Yeshua had committed any offense grave enough to merit punishment. But the Sanhedrin made a fuss about the heretic's violation of their sacred creed. So Pilatus, rather than risk another riot, gave in and let the fellow be crucified."

"What became of that Procurator?"

Panthera shrugged. "He was recalled to Rome when some people complained about him to the Emperor. You know how things are. Under the Empire, anyone who gets into a position of authority at once becomes the object of plots, conspiracies, and complaints, whether he has done anything wrong or not.

"Anyway, Pilatus survived until Emperor Tiberius died and Gaius, the crazy one, succeeded him. During that character's reign, Pilatus killed himself — though whether the mad Emperor ordered him to do so, or whether he simply got tired of life in imperial Rome, where everybody's hand is out for a bribe, I know not."

"What became of this Miriam?"

Panthera shrugged again. "No contact for many years. Twenty-odd years ago, I was quite besotted with her. I said I'd support her as my concubine until my hitch ended, and then I would legally marry her.

"You know, I suppose, that the divine Augustus ordained that soldiers may not marry during active service. The reasons they give for the law, such as the fact that soldiers can be ordered anywhere in the Empire, you probably know. But for individuals it can become damned inconvenient. One can for a small bribe, however, usually find a centurion willing to let the soldier and his woman go through some little local barbarian rite of marriage.

"I had just been promoted to *optio*, but even the extra pay didn't convince Miriam. No, the real objection was that I was of the *goyim*, the non-Jewish nations. A proper Jew looks down upon all such people much as we Greeks look down upon all non-Greeks as barbarians. Living in sin with a real Jew would have been bad enough; but with a 'gentile' it was out of the question.

"I even looked into the possibility of becoming a Jew myself. But I should have to spend endless hours studying their hairsplitting laws under one of their teachers, follow their complicated dietary rules, and undergo that disgusting mutilation of my personal parts that they insist on. Besides, since I couldn't prove direct descent from Abraham, it would make me only a second-class Jew and would interfere with my military duties. So my centurion would never allow it.

"So there we were. When we parted finally, she said she

really loved me, too; but the obstacles were imposed by their irascible god, Yahveh, and there was nothing to be done about it. She was going to Egypt, taking our little son with her, for she had heard that well-born Egyptian women don't go in for swarms of slaves the way Romans do. They will hire poor free women like her as housekeepers, to sweep and clean and make the beds and mind the children and wash the dishes. Besides, the city she was going to had a substantial Jewish settlement, with a temple and all. So that was that."

The centurion gave me a funny little crooked smile. "I sometimes wonder what would have happened if Miriam had remained in Judaea. I should have been — I suppose you might say — the stepfather of a demigod. It would be interesting to find out, but of course it's too late for that.

"I wonder, too, what would have happened if the Sixth had still been stationed in Judaea when young Yeshua and his mother came back from Egypt. I might have come to know the lad, and perhaps I could have steered him away from some of his impractical notions.

"Then again, perhaps not. You know how young men are, sure they know everything and that nothing a man of the older generation has to say could have anything to do with the real world of their own time.

"It might not have been so impossible if he had had a real, civilized education. But his upbringing had been narrowly Jewish. I'd wager he thought the world was flat and that he had never even heard of people like Aristotle and Demokritos, who investigated the world to find out how it actually worked."

"What of that carpenter Miriam was betrothed to before she took up with you?"

"I daresay he's long dead. He was a widower, old enough to be Miriam's father, with a houseful of children by his first wife. Needless to say, they would not have been friendly to me, or to young Yeshua either — though I believe that, after Yeshua's execution, one of that family, a certain Yakov, was converted to Yeshua's following and became a leader of the Jerusalem faction of the sect.

"This was not only after Yeshua's death, but also after that Jew from Tarsus, who Romanized his name to Paulus, went around preaching a complicated new theology to support the Yeshuites, or as they are now called, Christians, meaning followers of the Anointed One.

"This Paulus voyaged all over the Inner Sea, they say, carrying his message and starting up little groups of Christians in the cities he visited. He must have been a man of extraordinary energy and magnetic personality, though I confess the logic of his complex theology escapes me. But then, it seems likely that it would also escape anyone brought up on Aristotle, as I was. So I am sure these Christians will prove just one more little sect, which will soon fade away and be forgotten.

"Now tell me more about Maesius' business. I really

should not talk so much about my personal affairs. The barbarians say that the Greek national vice is not sodomy but garrulity.

"But about Maesius' business: You understand, of course, that I would not sign any hard-and-fast agreement on the basis of a conversation in a wine bar. I shall want to look around for other possibilities first."

Panthera was evidently a cautious fellow, which made him a likely partner for Maesius. The importer was getting old and did not have a son to break in to the business. After another hour, with the help of Herondas' wine, we had pretty much roughed out an agreement, provided that I could sell the idea to Maesius. He would of course want to meet Panthera himself before committing himself to anything.

And that, essentially, is how I came to be the factor for the partnership of Maesius and Panthera. When Maesius dies, Panthera has promised me his place. When the centurion became a full partner, he asked me not to discuss the tale of him and Miriam, on the ground that it would be bad for business.

"I've dealt with religious enthusiasts," he told me. "One thing I do know is that it does no good whatever to argue with them, no matter what evidence you adduce. They will brush it aside and sometimes go for you with a dagger, to punish you for casting slights on their sacred beliefs. If they kill you, Christians are sure the world is about to end any day now — certainly before Roman law could bring you to book. So what have they to lose?

"Can you imagine what it would do to the trade, with a squad of pious Jews screaming 'Heretics! Blasphemers!' at a squad of Christians, who scream back: 'Unbelievers! Atheists!' Then someone starts picking up our merchandise and throwing it…."

L. Sprague de Camp, one of the legendary masters of the fantasy and science fiction fields, authored such classics as "A Gun for Dinosaur" and the Harold Shea series (with Fletcher Pratt), and more than 120 other books. His tireless efforts as an editor (and posthumous collaborator) kept the works of Robert E. Howard alive through the 1960s and 1970s. He received the Gandalf Award, the Gramd Master Nebula Award, and many others.

AFTERWARD

by Clark Ashton Smith

There is a silence in the world
Since we have said farewell;
And beauty with an alien speech
An alien tale would tell.

There is a silence in the world,
Which is not peace nor quiet:
Ever I seek to flee therefrom,
And walk the ways of riot.

But when I hear the music moan
In rooms of thronging laughter,
A tongueless demon drives me forth,
And silence follows after.

THE LORD OF THE RAILS

by J.J. Travis

The pain in Logan's stomach wasn't just the result of bad food: anxiety and a sense of failure also had a hand in twisting his insides. He trudged through the camp, threadbare coat providing little warmth, cursing his stupidity for suggesting this assignment. Beck was proving to be unusually elusive; not that Logan had thought it would be a snap finding the man in this transient sea of discarded humanity, the neglected children of FDR's New Deal. And Beck certainly could not know he was being hunted.

Logan stopped at each campfire, discreetly searching the huddled packs of men (and, buried deep inside oversized men's clothing, the occasional woman) for Beck. Logan would know him when he saw him. He resisted the urge to linger by the warmth; the sooner he found Beck and finished his job, the sooner he'd be home. Unlike these poor souls he had a life to return to. He'd only been on this assignment for a week and he'd already seen and learned all he needed to know. He'd intended to focus primarily on Beck, a man of some power and position brought low. Beck would be the central theme, but there were other stories to tell. He'd seen first-hand the extent of the damage. He wondered if the country could recover.

Two years since the Black Friday of 1929 and the situation had never looked grimmer. And no end in sight. Just find Beck, get the story and get out.

And there he was. Beck sat with a group near the edge of the camp. He looked to be one of the streamliners, like Logan, traveling with minimum gear. All this searching and now Logan was afraid to approach the man. How to play this? The novice greenhorn, needing protection and a mentor? Well, he was new to this; that would be obvious.

He moved to the fire and stood for a moment warming his hands, then quietly sat at the edge of the group, away from Beck. The fire burned low. Eventually people began to scatter, turning in for the night. Beck and a few stragglers remained. Beck pulled a flask from his pocket and raised it in a salute to Logan. "Well, you finally found me."

Logan started.

"I beg your pardon?"

"Come come, lad. I remember you from my final press conference. Some insightful questions, if I recall."

"My God. I couldn't have made that much of an impression."

"I've lost much, my boy, but not my memory."

Logan moved next to him. "Not lost, perhaps; given up, I'd say. With people killing for jobs, you quit a secure and lucrative position for . . . this?"

"Higher calling, my boy. Serve a different god than Mammon now. Wasn't happy in my job, and all that."

"The Townsend incident have anything to do with it?"

"Well, in a way; yes, if you must know. It opened my eyes, that's for sure, got me to investigating. Changed my beliefs."

"So you're going to let me interview you, just like that."

"I haven't been avoiding you, dear boy. You seem to want to know so badly that I can't resist enlightening you. A bit flattering, actually; all that's going on in this country and you find *me* particularly interesting."

"I need angles. Put it on a personal level. I followed the Waters trial, talked to him. Found *his* story fascinating."

"You believed him? He was a writer of Gothics, young man. No stranger to spinning outlandish tales. I found his defense less credible than his fiction."

"Was it? Do you *still* believe that? You have to admit that the details surrounding Emily Townsend's death were bizarre: Waters's allegations, specifically concerning the Lewton-Arkham line and the Cartland Tunnel. The strange folklore and gossip about the tunnel and the area —"

"It was a crime of passion," Beck interrupted. "The young woman stood to inherit a fortune . . ."

"As Daniel Waters pointed out, she was his fiancee. Why murder her before they were married? He stood to gain nothing. And then there were the stories of *your* increasingly . . . eccentric behavior after the trial. Culminating in this . . ."

"Well, *finally* we come to me. What can I say? Pressures of the job and the negative publicity got to me." Beck smirked. "I could tell you the *real* story, but the question is: *Can you handle it?*"

"This is just a game to you."

"This is just a job to you. But no, it's more than an amusement. As I said before, it's a vocation. A calling."

"Being a hobo, riding the rails."

"Serving the Lord of the Rails."

"A metaphor for . . . ?"

"A reality. There are many gods. Some of them are insane. All of them are hungry. Many of them walk the earth, by choice or punishment. The Lord of the Rails is — if I may be blunt — a minor deity, but . . . accessible. Always looking for . . . acolytes. Well, servants, actually. Well, more like slaves, if you must know. I am one such humble slave.

Beats punching the time clock. You should try it."

Logan leaned close to Beck. "I've heard the name whispered; at first I thought it referred to *you*. Can I see this god?"

Beck grinned. "I was hoping you'd ask that! My Lord would enjoy meeting you. It likes people; positively relishes them. Savors the encounter."

It was Logan's turn to grin. "You make it sound like your god is going to eat me."

Beck looked startled. "Oh my; have I been obvious? I thought I was being clever and instead I just gave it away. Oh well, might as well fess up: the Lord *will* devour you."

Logan studied Beck, then shook his head. "That's it," Beck chuckled, "humor me, dear boy. My sense of humor is a bit twisted; insanity will do that to you."

Logan said, "So I can meet this god. In the flesh."

Beck patted him on the knee. "My boy, countless many have. Unlike Yahweh, my Lord is not afraid to show its faces. Do I scare you?"

"You are a bit . . . twitchy."

"Most enlightened people are; we're bursting with a knowledge denied the common herd. We want to share it. I can't wait to share you with the Lord of the Rails."

"So your god requires its 'slaves' to ride the rails and . . .'"

"No, not preach the gospel. Only to show a few deserving souls the path to . . . the Lord. Guess I'm still in public relations, of a sort. I'm good with faces, but not names, Mr. —"

"Logan."

"Mr. Logan. Isn't this a more substantial story than another generic 'this country's going to hell in a handwagon' piece? If you're willing; if you feel you can accept it. And yes, it will vindicate your Mr. Waters: though it's far too late to benefit him."

"And I can write this story? Tell it true?"

"You may not want to. You can't face a god and remain unchanged. Will your petty job matter anymore? Can you handle that? Is knowledge of that scope worth the sacrifice?"

"You tell me."

"I'll do better: I'll show you. We'll have to hop the southbound later tonight. My Lord ranges far in its territory; but it prefers to dwell in the high country. It's a natural climber. I believe its place of origin is a plateau in China. Or is it Tibet? I'm not sure; the Lord isn't one for small talk."

"You keep calling this god 'Lord', denoting male gender, yet you keep referring to it as 'it'."

Beck took a swig from his flask. "Well, it's not human. Don't know its gender, or if it has one. Seems an impertinent question to ask a god. Oh yes, the Lord is most definitely an *it*. It has a name, though I have trouble pronouncing it when I'm sober, let alone drunk, which I am now.

Told you I wasn't good with names."

Beck urinated against a tree. "You found me in a *week*?"

Logan shifted his weight to work a kink out of his back. "Played a hunch. An article about life on the rails mentioned that you were known to travel the Lewton-Arkham circuit regularly. You'd been seen repeatedly."

"Ah. A hobo celebrity, am I? Irony in there somewhere."

"And you have a reputation."

"Really?"

"Among the regulars. They call you the shepherd. Their attitude implies fear."

Beck sat next to Logan. "Oh dear. I'm no religious zealot. Nothing to fear from me. I serve my Lord. These poor souls with their shattered, meaningless lives have nothing. I introduce them to a wonder, something beyond the scope of their bland existence. That frightens people."

"Many regulars are afraid to travel this line. Sound familiar?"

Beck farted. "Pardon. The Waters incident intrigued me. I did some personal as well as official investigating. I found the folklore concerning the Lewton-Arkham line and the area around the Cartland Tunnel to be rooted in fact. I became a believer. This was after Waters's trial, my boy, so don't mark me as the villain. I 'uncovered' the Lord, confronted it. We struck a bargain. I bring in the lambs for the flock."

"And what does your god do for you?"

"Lets me live. I promised that if the Lord spared me I would serve it. Same deal the ancients struck with Yahweh. I know what a mundane cliche this seems, but that's the way life is. Life is banal, life is simple: Serve or be served up. Of course the drugs help."

"I beg your pardon?"

Beck grinned.

"To ensure my cooperation the Lord injected me with its venom. Too small a dose to be lethal, but a potent narcotic. *Very* addictive. Ah, this is it. Listen."

Logan heard the distant sound of an approaching freight train. Beck started to rise but Logan grabbed his arm and pulled him down. "I'm a lamb being led to slaughter, aren't I?"

Beck jerked free of Logan's grip. "No, no, boy, I promise you won't be hurt. I told you I need to share this knowledge. I can't keep doing this forever; the Lord understands this. And you *need* to know, don't you? Now hurry!"

Beck stood and gestured for Logan to follow. They waited behind a tree near the tracks. "There are always a few empty open cars on this leg of the route," Beck said. "Just do as I do."

The freight came into view and slowed as it took a turn. Logan looked around and saw that they were alone; no one else from the camp seemed to be joining them.

"*Now!*" Beck shouted as he ran for the train. Logan noted that the hard life seemed to have rejuvenated the older man. Or maybe it was from the juice of the god that supposedly pumped through him. Logan struggled to keep up with Beck as they ran alongside one of the open boxcars.

Beck swerved and grabbed the door side, hauled himself up and reached out a hand to help pull Logan aboard.

The two men lay panting for breath. The boxcar swayed mercilessly; it was useless to try to gain footing. They crawled to a corner and huddled in the darkness. Flashes of moonlight through the trees revealed that they were alone.

Logan felt for the bottle of alcohol in his coat pocket and checked it; it hadn't shattered. He hated the dark and instinctively reached for the box of matches in his other pocket. He struck a match.

Beck eyed him with amusement. "Once we hit the open country the moonlight will provide sufficient illumination."

"Is it far?"

"Few hours."

Logan did not light another match. "No bulls or yard dicks?"

"No headcrackers on *this* run. You'll see why."

Logan tried to make himself comfortable and adjust to the noise. He could never acclimatize himself to the constant barrage of sensation on a freight, the ceaseless, mind-numbing motion and clatter. He supposed one got used to it over time; he did not intend to find out. "I don't have any money. If this is an elaborate ruse to jump me, it won't be profitable."

"It always is, one way or another," Beck answered. "You'll have a story like no other. You will know. Can't guarantee you'll be better for the knowledge. If you're like all the others I've shared this with, you'll curse my existence till your dying breath. The human mind is not designed to handle *everything*."

"I'm prepared to believe." Logan could not see Beck in the dark.

"You ran the Arkham Central Railroad. As president, you must have traveled these lines. You must have known —"

"Foolish rumors," Beck interrupted. "The Lord was in a dormant state. Ancient gods hibernate for ages; sleep, troubled sleep, restless, unquiet. The Lord began to stir again about the time of the Waters affair. The Lord wasn't responsible for Emily Townsend's death. There are other things: Parasites, ticks from the Lord's hide; loathsome abominations. One of them crawled through an open window and fed on her. Since Waters was sleeping in the same compartment he was the logical suspect and was 'railroaded' into a conviction. Railroaded. I like that. The two not yet married, sleeping in the same compartment. *Shocking.*"

Logan clenched his teeth and fists in anger. He heard Beck moving closer in the darkness. Intermittent flashes of

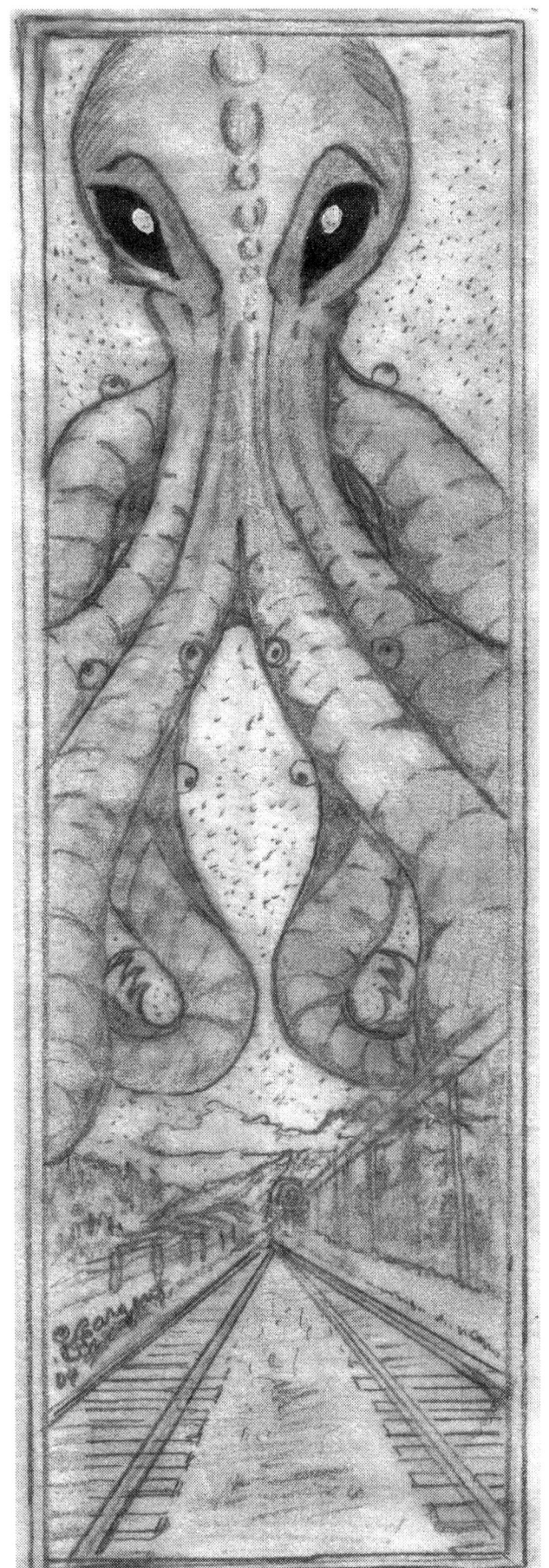

moonlight revealed Beck kneeling next to him. The older man leaned against the wall and sighed.

"I hate this part. The waiting. I'm between worlds. In the camps I can lose myself among humanity, dirty as it is. There's still some of the old me left; enough to care sometimes. And when I'm in the overwhelming presence of the Lord, my devotion is absolute. But this middle ground — when I'm left to myself — it's . . . hard. I don't like my company. I'm very tired now. Rest. Wait for the whistle."

The freight's speed picked up and the increased noise made talk difficult. The train slowly gained altitude; unfiltered moonlight illuminated the dark, rolling hills. Logan lost track of time. The incessant monotony of the journey allowed him to occasionally doze.

Logan snapped awake, glanced over to see Beck awake and sitting up, hugging himself against the cold. Beck stared at the doorway, seemingly mesmerized by the passing terrain. "We're in the Lord's favored territory, near the Place of Meeting. In a moment we'll pass through the tunnel and the Great Old One will drop in for a visit."

Logan tensed. "I'm not like the others," he told Beck. "I *believe*. I accept the monstrous. My line of work makes it easy."

Beck turned to him and smiled. "You say that now. Come face to face with something primal, something of the *other*, there's no way to prepare for that."

"Certain emotions harden one: anger. Hate."

The whistle sounded, startling Logan. Total darkness enveloped them. "Ah, the tunnel!" Beck shouted unnecessarily.

The tone of the train changed as it passed through the tunnel, the ghostly whistle the shriek of something lost in the darkness, the clatter reverberating off the walls like repeating gunfire.

"I lied," Beck's gloating voice said from the dark. "You *will* be hurt. Horribly."

They were coming out of the tunnel. The moment their car cleared it something landed on the roof. Beck looked up. "Our honored guest has arrived."

Logan breathed deeply and rapidly, near hyperventilation. He fought to calm himself. *Was* he ready for this? He heard weakened timbers buckle and snap as something heavy moved across the roof toward the open doorway. He reached into his pocket and pulled out the bottle.

Beck leaned close and smirked. "The Lord doesn't drink. And that's no weapon against a god."

Logan punched Beck in the face. The older man fell back and lay still. Logan unscrewed the bottle cap with shaky fingers and dumped some of the contents on Beck's head and shoulders. He reached into his pants pocket and pulled out a strip of cloth; he stuffed it in the neck of the bottle and fumbled for the box of matches.

Beck groaned and stirred. Logan was preparing to punch him again when his attention was caught by a movement near the doorway.

Something long and thin snaked into the car. Logan moaned and froze. He struggled to comprehend what he was seeing in the weak moonlight. The inhumanly long, thin appendage was reaching in from the roof outside, groping for purchase. He defined the limb as an arm or leg, ebony skin desiccated and parched dry; the limb tapered off to end in three long, sharp-nailed claws or toes. The nails hooked into the doorside wood and gouged deep. Another limb dropped down to grasp the other side of the doorway.

Logan whimpered. He had to look away, or he was dead. He propped the bottle between his thighs and concentrated on opening the box of matches. Beck was stirring again.

Logan looked up and screamed. The Lord of the Rails had pulled itself into the boxcar, filling the doorway and blocking out most of the moonlight. It cocked its misshapen head and seemed to gaze upon Logan. Logan screamed harder. Mercifully, the Lord's features weren't clear in the darkness, saving Logan's sanity. He had a quick impression of multiple faces, none of them remotely human, many eyes and mouths, all focused on him. The Lord hovered by the doorway, swaying with the motion of the train and its own sinuous, serpentine movement.

Beck cackled and tried to sit up. Still groggy, he started to crawl toward Logan. Logan kicked out and caught Beck in the forehead with his boot. Beck rolled on his side and curled up.

Logan shot a glance at the silent black thing in the doorway. Scarecrow-thin body and segmented limbs were still; the snouted, many-jawed faces watched his every movement. The Lord's arms were long enough for it to reach out and grab him from where it crouched, but it did nothing. Many ancient eyes, but could they see him clearly? Ancient. *Old*. Too old to be an effective predator? Was this god dependent on Beck for its survival? The thought energized Logan with hope.

Beck got his second wind and started for Logan again. "So many innocents," Logan said as he fumbled a wooden match from the box. "Starting with Emily Townsend and Daniel Waters. Poor, sweet Emily."

Beck stopped; he seemed surprised at Logan's sanity and relative composure. He glanced at his god; certainly the Lord feared nothing, but still it hesitated. And Logan, going on and on about Daniel Waters, obsessed with the man. Something not right here. The Lord was waiting for him to act, to right the situation. "I told you that Waters was making a big noise," Beck said. "Had to sacrifice him. Is *that* what triggered this grand quest of yours? You interviewed him and believed his insane story?"

Logan struck the match. "I didn't say I interviewed him; I said I talked to him. And *yes,* I believed him." Logan touched the match to the strip of cloth. It ignited instantly.

He held the bottle up. Beck could see the tears on Logan's face. "He was my brother."

Logan climbed to his feet and hurled the bottle at the Lord of the Rails. The bottle of pure grain alcohol shattered against the hide of the Lord; flames quickly spread and engulfed the god. There was enough illumination to see the beast clearly, but its features were consumed by the flames. There were things the size of cats that crawled across the burning flesh: the ticks Beck had mentioned. They flew out the doorway on flaming wings. The flames hissed; the silent god thrashed and reared back.

Beck screamed and fumbled for something in his pocket. Logan moved to him and kicked him in the face; the derringer dropped from Beck's hand. Logan jerked him to his feet and pushed him across the car toward the Lord of the Rails. Flaming limbs reached out and grabbed Beck. He burst into flames as his god embraced him. Locked in a frenzied dance, the flailing mass tumbled out the door.

Logan fell and crawled to the doorway. Two burning forms separated and rolled down the steep hill.

Logan began to shake and weep. He had enough wits left to stamp out the small straw fires before his brain caught up with the facts and shut down.

Logan was unconscious when the freight pulled into its last stop. He came to when one of the yard bulls pulled him out. Before he could react the bull put a knot in Logan's skull with his sap. Logan was grateful for the return to temporary oblivion.

He would write his story. There would be no mention of Beck or monstrous demon gods.

Hard times and meaningless lives. What of it? Maybe there are true gods; Logan can't say for certain. He knows there are devils.

J.J. Travis celebrated his twentieth year of publication in 2004. He has received three honorable mentions in The Year's Best Fantasy and Horror. *He has another tale coming out in* All Hallows. *The present story stands on its own but also follows as a sequel to* "Down the Line" *in* Whispers from a Shattered Forum *(1997).*

THE MESSENGER

by H. P. Lovecraft

The thing, he said, would come in the night at three
From the old churchyard on the hill below;
But crouching by an oak fire's wholesome glow,
I tried to tell myself it could not be.

Surely, I mused, it was pleasantry
Devised by one who did not truly know
The Elder Sign, bequeathed from long ago,
That sets the fumbling forms of darkness free.

He had not meant it - no - but still I lit
Another lamp as starry Leo climbed
Out of the Seekonk, and a steeple chimed
Three - and the firelight faded, bit by bit.

Then at the door that cautious rattling came -
And the mad truth devoured me like a flame!

FROM THE PITS
OF ELDER BLASPHEMY

by Hugh B. Cave

There were drums tonight — or was it thunder, so far off he couldn't yet tell the difference? But then he could hardly hear them. Not only too far off, but suddenly drowned by something closer at hand, something admittedly less ominous, but with more raw irritation — the barking of dogs. It started, his bedside clock documented, at precisely 3:15 in the morning, putting an end to any hope of slumber. One dog would bark somewhere in that part of Port-au-Prince in which he had rented a room at the Pension Etoile. Half a dozen others would follow, scattered throughout the city, at first with an almost tentative note, as if a great canine orchestra were tuning up for a concert. But when they started in earnest, it was more like a shouting match, each bark answered by challenging rejoinders until the whole city was set ahowl. Dismissing the momentary urge to add his own barked "Quiet!" to the melee, a weary Peter Macklin gave up in disgust and got out of bed. Shrugging himself into his clothes, he opened the verandah door to let in any breeze that might be passing by. It was July, and Haiti — this Caribbean land of *vodun* and poverty — was as savagely hot as its people were gentle in their unspoken surrender.

He had expected the city to be hot in July, of course. As a graduate student of anthropology, that fascinating study of man's veiled origins, struggling development, and kaleidoscopic cultures, he had twice before visited Haiti to write about *vodun* and its believers. By now he could speak enough French to carry on conversations with the country's elite, as well as sufficient Creole to communicate with the masses. And he had had ample occasion in his work to do both. His studies had evidenced enough early promise to merit a modest travel stipend included as part of his scholarship, but it was close to exhausted, and he had comparatively little to show for it. After all, *vodun*, "voodoo," had long attracted researchers, both serious and sensationalist, because of its inherent exoticism, and his academic advisors warned him of delving into a dried-up well. He was beginning to fear they had been right. What else was there to say about it?

This time he was here on little more than a hunch, based on a rumor he had heard in Miami's Little Haiti while visiting his parents in Florida. He had once heard of something similar in hushed whispers among the Rasta communities of Jamaica, too. The rumor involved certain of the magicians, or shamans, as anthropologists were careful to call them nowadays, *bocors* and *houngans*, belonging to a secret cult whose members were in touch with unknown deities, terrible gods from the sound of it, who might be called upon to do terrible things. The infamous zombie legends went back to such people. They existed as religious outlaws on the margins of *vodun* society and theology, operating much as contract killers who claimed magical means to do dirty jobs. But until now no one had ever heard of them banding together in a religious society of their own. Was it something new? Or perhaps something very, very old, only now becoming known for the first time? In either case, here was a new wrinkle, a new aspect of the matter. And his research took on a whole new relevance. Here was his chance not only to avoid reploughing a depleted field, but even to gain a precocious reputation among his peers by a major discovery. If, that is, he could make it more than a rumor. There would have to be interviews, participant observation, and before that — some actual, personal contact.

And here he was in luck, for it turned out that the brother of a young Haitian in Florida, who did odd jobs for Peter's family, claimed association with this mysterious cult, and Peter was awaiting the arrival of this man, one Metellus Dalby, who would bring him news of the group's latest meeting. He did not have long to wait. It almost seemed as though the barking of the sleepless dogs had been prophetic, an oracle wrung from them by some supernatural influence on their keen other-than-human senses. Within fifteen minutes there came a knock on the rickety door of his room.

Leaving the little verandah where he had gone for a breath of air, only to find more of the crowded city's suffocating heat, Peter advanced the short distance to the door and opened it. The man confronting him was a Haitian, tall, slender, and very black.

"You're back already?" asked Peter, startled, in Creole. It came out almost like a rebuke.

"With good news, *m'sieu*." Nodding briskly, Metellus Dalby stepped past him into the room, then spun about to face him. "There is to be a big meeting of the cult this very night. You must accompany me to it!"

The bright gibbous moon illuminated the scene of two men, one white, one black, staring at each other. Then the Haitian spoke again, more slowly. "But there is something we must do first, *mon ami*." From a pocket of his baggy trousers he withdrew a pint bottle of some dark liquid.

Peter nodded. "How long will it take?"

"I will apply the first coat now, another about noon, and a third before we begin the journey." His smile broadened into a shining crescent moon. "You will look like one of my people when I finish, I promise you that. And while it will itch, a little, it will not inconvenience you."

"What about my sharp nose, my thin lips?" For the first time, Peter saw them as he feared a non-Caucasian might see them, not handsome, but marks of alien origin.

"Haitians come in all shapes, my friend. Some of our ladies on the Mardi Gras floats could win prizes anywhere in the world. You've seen them."

The Pension Etoile was on the Champ de Mars, and, that being part of the Mardi Gras route, Peter involuntarily glanced out the window, as if half-expecting to see the marching bands and gaudy floats in full force. His companion smiled again, showing those whiter than white teeth.

"It may burn a little, this vegetable dye," Metellus warned. "But not for long. You'll be comfortable again soon, I promise." Peter wondered what sort of errands had made Metellus so familiar with the stuff and its use. Whatever they might have been, they only made Metellus exactly the sort of person who would know how to help him on a gambit such as he contemplated. Like the CIA, anthropologists sometimes had to deal with people who could get things done when there were only dubious ways to get them done.

Peter took the two or three steps to the bed, removed the top part of his pajamas, and lay down on his back. Pulling the cork from the bottle and leaning like a masseuse over his client, this man he looked on more and more as a friend, Metellus began the process of darkening those parts of the white man's body that would be revealed by short-sleeved attire. As he did so, he talked.

"What is to happen tonight, *m'sieu*, will interest you, I am certain. These people plan a special meeting in which they will call upon the Old Ones to present themselves. There is a line you will hear, and you must be ready to join in the first time you hear it. 'That is not dead which can eternal lie, and with strange eons, even death may die.' I heard it from Tiburon, on the Southern Peninsula, who told me it was not for the ears of just anyone. You do not want to sound like it is new to you. That is not dead," he repeated, coachingly, "which can eternal lie, and with strange eons, even death may die."

"Meaning?" Peter asked with a frown.

The Haitian shrugged. "Who knows, exactly? But they know its meaning, never fear. And perhaps after tonight we, too, shall know." He fell silent, giving the white man

the chance to repeat the formula to himself silently till he knew it.

When the bottle was empty, Metellus stepped back from the bed to look Peter over, then nodded. "We should plan on being there before dark, so we can show my work off to best advantage, eh? We can use my Jeep to take us as far as Furcy, then we'll have to walk a few miles. Those mountain trails are not easy, as I believe you know."

Paying as little mind as he could to his tingling skin, Peter looked at the mirror while speaking to his partner. "What time did you leave there tonight?"

"Just after midnight."

Peter glanced at an alarm clock on his chest of drawers, subtracting the minutes it was off by. Its lazy hands now stood at five minutes to five, and Metellus had been here how long? Forty-five minutes? A little more? "So we want to be there when?"

"I should plan on picking you up about three o'clock this afternoon, I think."

Nodding matter-of-factly, Peter opened the top of the chest of drawers, a storage place with absolutely no security, to take out his billfold. From it he handed the Haitian some gourd notes. "Fill up the gas tank, Metellus. Better put some food in the Jeep as well. There's no telling what we may be getting into, eh?"

"Thanks, boss," he answered with a note of irony, noticing that there was more there than needed for the tasks Peter had stipulated. He left, and Peter's sole companion was once again the humidity, which by now seemed to have gotten the better of the dogs, who had fallen silent. Maybe he'd be able to get some sleep now. When the dye on his skin seemed to be dry enough, Peter returned to his bed and dozed till mid-morning, knowing he would probably not sleep at all in the night ahead of him. Who or what, he wondered, were the "Old Ones" his Haitian friend had talked about? Old gods, older than the conventional Obeah pantheon, to be sure. But which gods? What kind? It later seemed vaguely to him that his dreams that morning tried to give him some hint, but he could not remember.

Come five minutes to three that afternoon, Metellus turned his Jeep into the Pension driveway, and Peter, standing ready, stepped right into it. Several of the little hotel's other guests had stared unabashedly at Peter as he had descended the staircase from his second-floor room and walked through the downstairs hall to the door. No doubt they were startled at a white man having becoming a black one, but none questioned him, perhaps feeling it safer not to. As he slid onto the seat beside the driver's, his Haitian friend nodded approval and said, "The dye worked well, I see. If I were you, I might be wondering how long it will take to wear off."

"I have thought about it, now that you mention it." Peter smiled as he made himself as comfortable as possible.

FROM THE PITS OF ELDER BLASPHEMY

The Jeep was an old one, open, with a fabric top to shield its two occupants from rain or sun.

"You may continue to be a Haitian for three or four days," said Metellus, with the air of a doctor, showing his white teeth again in a grin.

"I can think of things I'd less rather be."

"Eh?"

Peter realized he probably hadn't phrased the remark properly in Creole. "Just so long as it works tonight," he amended.

"Yes," replied Metellus with surprising and sudden gravity, as he backed out of the Pension's drive. "Just so long as the Old Ones don't know who and what you really are." Peter thought about that remark from time to time as the two of them traveled up the winding road to Petionville, where so many of the country's wealthier citizens lived to escape the heat and squalor of Haiti's capital. It lingered in his mind on the even longer climb over a narrow blacktop road to the mountain village of Kenscoff. And it jabbed at his mind now and then as Metellus, a skilled and careful driver, took the little vehicle up the final twisting climb to the end of the driving road at Furcy. At various times during the journey Peter had turned in his seat to peer down through the heat-haze hanging over the roofs of the capital, as if trying to penetrate the opaque mists of antiquity. He wondered why he was doing what he was doing. Did all anthropologists live dangerously? It was only missionaries who wound up in cooking pots, wasn't it?

His companion brought the vehicle to a stop in front of a peasant cottage, and Peter snapped out of his reverie. "We leave the Jeep here," Metellus announced. "These people know me." He glanced at the watch on his wrist. Peter had earlier observed that he wore a Rolex or some such, which one would think out of the range of any legitimate income. But he had wisely traded it for a more modest Timex for the occasion. "Are you hungry, my friend?"

His eyes concluding a sweep of the cottage and what lay beyond it, Peter barely caught the words but replied, "I hadn't given it a thought. The heat takes away my appetite. But perhaps we ought to eat something, eh?"

Metellus slid from his seat and leaned into the back of the Jeep to lift out a bag of food. It turned out to be a strange mixture of fruit, vegetables, and the worst sort of greasy junk food. More of all of it than they could expect to eat. And there was alcohol. Metellus opened the bag and gave him his choice. Peter grabbed a couple of apples and a roll. Metellus took even less. Just then the cottage door opened, and it was an attractive, middle-aged black woman who greeted them both with a smile and a happy "Bon jour!" Metellus handed her the rest of the provisions. Trust him to think of everything, Peter thought.

From there they walked. And Peter soon discovered and appreciated why Metellus had judged it wise to arrive at their destination before dark. The trail was a footpath. It was a snake twisting through the forest. At times it would be blocked by fallen tree-limbs, mostly pine, and by boulders that must have come crashing down the mountain. Peter hoped there were no more like them at home. It seemed endless.

Peter was tired, his companion scarcely less so, when the pair finally arrived at a cluster of huts in a clearing that, mercifully, turned out to be their destination. But there was to be no rest for them. People came striding from the huts — men, mostly — and Peter had to be introduced to them by Metellus. Had to smile and remain standing while his companion explained that Peter was a Floridian, a friend of Metellus' brother, and that he was deeply interested in the Old Ones. Also that he was eager to participate in the night's proceedings, at least as an observer. Peter momentarily started at hearing the exact truth from the other's lips. He had expected more pretense than this, though he could think of no real reason it should be necessary.

By the time the newcomer had been introduced all around, it had grown dark enough for lanterns to be lit and hung in the surrounding trees, and *vodun* drums began to throb. No one seemed suspicious of him, and the only looks in his direction that he noticed appeared to be polite and friendly. He returned the smiles he saw and hoped for the best. He asked if he might do anything to help prepare, was told that he was a guest and should not busy himself with such tasks. This he took for permission to nod off for a brief nap.

Once he felt Metellus nudging him awake, he realized he had slept for at least three hours. The moon was high, and the clearing was now crowded with eager figures darting to and fro, creating almost a strobe effect as they passed rapidly before the blazing lamps and lanterns. He got rapidly to his aching feet and looked nervously to make sure his sleeping posture had not revealed any pink flesh. Metellus's grin anticipated him and let him know all was well. The two of them hurried into the circle and looked for good seats, close to the action, whatever action there should be, yet not too obtrusive, lest any surprise or reluctance on their part be noticed. Here at the scene itself, Peter wondered for the first time how much of the celebrations of this sect Metellus had actually seen? He spoke enigmatically about it, as if he knew little, and yet he appeared to be well enough known to those gathered. Perhaps he had received only a preliminary degree of initiation and could only guess, as Peter had heard him do, at the real secrets of the cult. But didn't that imply he himself, an outsider, could not hope to see anything much out of the ordinary? Well, there was nothing to do but wait now.

He scanned the close-packed crowd. The scene was familiar, as were the expressions of adventurous expectancy on the black faces gleaming with sweat and firelight. Then with a start he hoped no one noticed, he saw faces of a more ominous cast, weathered and haughty visages whose peculiar lines betrayed habitual emotions and exaltations of a kind he could not guess. Some bore ritual scars, others faded tattoos and paint. There were ear-hoops of strange workmanship, too, some suggesting the forms of strange sea creatures. Here was something new. Might he perhaps interview these old men, who were certainly those curiously allied *bocors* and *houngans* rumor had described as improbably coming together for some frightful purpose? He sensed somehow his chances of that were slim.

His eagerness dulled to disappointment once the congregation hushed as if by some tacit signal and the service began. The celebrant, an aged fellow with a wrinkled face and a voice little more than a fatigued whisper, droned out the singsong of the usual introductory prayers. He drew the usual *veves* around the base of the central pole or *poteau mitan*. Still droning, as if wearily reciting a child's nursery rhyme, he called upon the usual string of *vodun* deities: Legba, Ogoun, Erzulie, Damballah, and the rest. Peter had seen and heard all this too many times before. And yet the gathered cultists appeared to be all the more eager, as if their favorite part were on its way.

At once the rote character of the display vanished. The preliminaries, perfunctory, were over. Gestures in the crowd became rapid, even violent, aimless jabs, striking heads and torsos oblivious of the impact. Eyes rolled up, people blindly rising, shrilly chanting, joining a frenzied follow-the-leader snake-dance. At Metellus' urgent signal, Peter joined in as best he could. He strained to make out the words being sung, and because of the number of voices, twenty-five or so, it was difficult. Especially difficult for one to whom Creole was not a primary language. Yet he understood some of it. And to his surprise, these black bacchantes were calling not on the traditional gods of *vodun*, whose names he had heard mere moments before, but on someone, something, far more ancient. The names were altogether new to him, and he realized this was why it was so difficult to understand. Some of the . . . names? . . . were so bizarre, and were barked and screamed past comprehension. *Tulu . . . Nigguratl-Yig . . . Nug* and *Yeb . . .* And the cacophony was rapidly giving way to some alien language, perhaps speaking in tongues. Less and less Creole.

An intuitive flash told him what must be going on here. Old Ones. He knew, anyone knew, that the nominal Christianity of Haitians and other Caribbean peoples thinly masked the African religions of their pre-slavery ancestors. They might call the object of their ecstatic devotion Saint This or That, but they were really invoking Damballah, Baron Samedhi and the others, gods of ancient Africa. But what he was beholding here was something else — these Old Ones had to be the unthinkably archaic gods and devils to whom screaming sacrifices had been offered in the dawn ages before Zimbabwe and Benin and Opar, deities whose worship had at length been banned and driven

underground to take refuge under the names of the more wholesome gods of Zulu, Ashanti, Shona, and other tribes. Behind their myths the Things of Elder Blasphemy still lurked and ravened, as the benign spirits of African faiths would later hide behind the haloes of Catholic saints. In a moment he knew.

The chanting and the drumming continued. So did the dancing, as the cultists formed a rough circle and continued to move their feet — some in flat-soled sandals, others quite bare — in a shuffling processional. The celebrant, whose torpor had long since vanished, hopped into the center of the circle and began to rotate, his glazed eyes following the crowd as it spun round him. He shouted something once, twice, stabbing a finger in the direction of two of the entranced mob. One of these, who could hardly have even been aware of the summons, a teen-aged girl, broke from the group and fell to the ground. She was instantly followed by a second, this one an old hag. Further uncouth vocables erupted from the voodoo priest's raw throat, and the two females obediently threw off all restraint, their faces still strangely vacant, and began a savage death-struggle. Gouts of blood and torn-off flesh flew everywhere, and Peter's stomach roiled. Fistfuls of human meat, an eye, another, scattered into the air. Blood somehow splashed over him from the direction of the two women as if thrown from a paint can. The young anthropologist found his consciousness tottering. Rousing a moment later, he realized he had fallen into the arms of Metellus. He prayed no one else had noticed this failure of nerve, but a quick glance told him no one was paying any attention to him, nor would they.

Parts of the two ragged forms surrounded the old priest, who now sank to his bony knees and began to scoop up the blood and apply it to himself, a gory baptism, finally falling down and rolling in the crimson pool. The others grew silent, watching intently, Metellus and Peter no less than the rest. The old man regained his knees and remained in a posture of supplication, his blank eyes showing only their whites, intoning some throat-kinking chant

Peter knew that in an ordinary *vodun* ritual, one would next expect the ecstatic possession trances to begin, nothing very sinister, not far removed from the goings-on in any Appalachian Pentecostal ceremony. But he was in for a surprise. From one of the nearby huts a strange figure appeared. The crowd wheeled as one to face it. The drummers poised motionless with hands upraised over their drumheads. Into the clearing there slowly advanced, on clawlike feet each some fifteen inches long, a body like that of a chicken but as big as a barrel, with the head of a human male. And it did not seem to be a costume. Behind it in single file came half a dozen other monstrosities. In absolute silence (Peter absently noted the distant cacchinations of forest insects) the cultists widened their circle to give the summoned newcomers enough room.

Then came another, all by itself. A creature Peter Macklin recognized from his reading, or thought he did. What was its name? He could not remember. His mind was in too much of a turmoil to function properly. But the thing was like an octopus. A huge one. You couldn't see all of it because it seemed to sprout a number of weaving, waving tentacles. They moved with supreme ease despite the lack of any fluid medium. Everything about it seemed to be in motion, hypnotic motion. Some of the tentacles moved it forward; others writhed and trembled above its bulbous body, glistening greasily in the lantern light that illumined the whole clearing. Then as it came closer Peter saw that he had been wrong; in truth it was more like a huge sea-serpent, with ugly-looking big claws on some of its arms — or were the arms really feet? All he knew for sure was that a name for it came into his mind.

The monstrous Thing joined those that had preceded it. It was no longer certain what was or was not hallucination. To Peter it somehow appeared that he was looking at a line of gigantic creatures seen from a great distance. But then they seemed to be standing here, with their human worshippers, in this Haitian hilltop clearing. Metellus, beside Peter, now on his left, leaned toward his companion, who was plainly paling beneath the dye. He said in a low voice, "That last one is the dreaded *Tulu*, my friend."

The name which had come into Peter's mind was different. It was Cthulhu. But he only nodded. And then he felt two pairs of strong hands take his elbows and guide him quickly out of the circle and into one of the huts, not that from which the entities had emerged. Momentarily, amid his sudden panic, it occurred to Peter to wonder how any of the tiny huts could have contained the great creatures he saw. A familiar voice spoke in the intelligible accents of Creole. It was Metellus.

"Do not worry. The ceremony has reached a point which we may not see. Here, take your rest." Metellus indicated a soft straw mat on the ground. Peter felt himself sinking fast into sleep. Perhaps he had in truth been hypnotized, or perhaps the emotional shocks he had experienced were proving too much for him. He put up no resistance. He did not notice whether Metellus lay down beside him or returned to the festivities.

Peter slept dreamlessly, or at least he remembered no dreams, and this with a strange sense of relief. He was awakened by the hand shaking his shoulder. He was led wordlessly by a couple of big Haitians into another of the huts. There, cross-legged and completely cleansed of the previous night's defilements, sat the wizened priest, who silently motioned him to sit on the ground opposite him. His two retainers assumed waiting positions on either side of the structure, seeming to blend in with the barbaric figures depicted on hangings that draped the circular walls. Peter felt no fear, only a sense of nervous anticipation, much as he had felt defending his Master's thesis before his

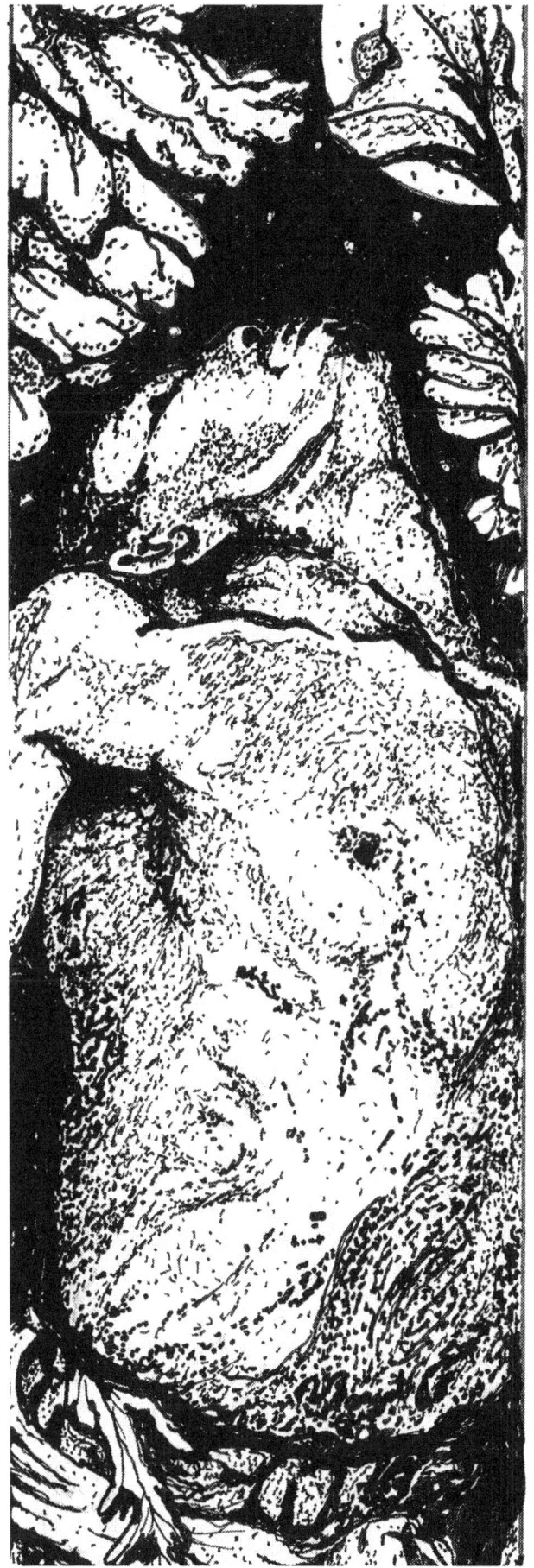

committee.

The old man's Creole was clear, his voice steady. "Young sir, I think you would like to join us. Have you not come among us for that purpose? A simple initiation will be required. Don't worry. No harm will come to you, despite what you perhaps think that you witnessed last night. Then, and only then, can our true secrets be revealed to you."

Peter did not hesitate. Indeed, this was more than he could have hoped for! He had seen something disturbing the previous night, at least he thought he had. But he could not remember what. Maybe he had dreamed after all. At any rate, this would be an unparalleled opportunity for participant observation. This was his chance to do original research into a virtually unknown Afro-Caribbean religion! His academic career would be off to a flying start!

"It would be an honor, Grandfather. I must tell you, though, I must eventually return to the States where I have obligations. I would not be able to be present as regularly as I would desire. May I still join you?"

"Your friend Metellus has told us you would divide your time between here and the United States. That poses no difficulty. You bring to us new blood. I believe your coming to be a boon both to yourself and to our divine lords. Indeed, I have no doubt but that it is they who guided your path to us."

Peter smiled and answered, "I'm sure you are right, Grandfather." He secretly wondered how delighted the old man or any of the others would be when he published his research on their cult. He hated to betray a confidence in that way, but it was sometimes necessary if knowledge were to be shared with one's colleagues, and with the world.

"Go and rest now, young Peter, till tonight, when you shall swear the First Oath of Damballah. Remain in your hut until the sun sets. Then these brethren (indicating the two giants who still stood silently like sculptures) will pick you up for the ceremony, when you will become one with us." He smiled. Both men rose. Which man was concealing more from the other?

When he returned, Peter was glad to see Metellus waiting for him.

"Tonight I'm to be initiated, Met!"

"Me, too," the Haitian replied, making his friend's eyes widen.

"I half-suspected you were already a member, the way everybody knows you here."

"The truth is that I took the First Oath when a young boy. I took the Second when I reached manhood, at age thirteen. I learned more then than you know now. But the Deep Things, as they call them, are revealed only to those who take the Third Oath of Damballah. That is what I'm to take tonight. I hoped I would. But now I'm beginning to wonder, to worry. I think maybe I've already seen too much."

"You mean, last night?"

"Yes, that's exactly what I mean. Except that I don't know what I mean. I can't remember much, except for some nightmares afterwards. I don't know what was dream and what wasn't. Do you?" Peter shook his head, a frown settling across his stained face.

"I'm not sure I want to go through with it, Peter. And I'm even less sure you ought to go through with it."

"But why not, Met? It seems like a once-in-a-lifetime opportunity!"

"Oh, it is — for them!"

"I don't follow you."

"About the only thing they don't know about you, *mon ami*, is that you are white. I doubt they would care about that any more. You see, I think they want to use you, your position in society back in the States. They know that you will have connections they could never get, influence they wish they had."

"For what?"

"Oh, the cult is very old. They once had power and influence on a scale you can't imagine. They would love to get it back. At least that's what the Old Ones are telling them in dreams. I know, because since the Second Oath, I share in some of those dreams. And they think you can help them get their old power back again. And I'll tell you something else — I'm quite sure they'll never let you publish the facts of what's really going on here. Only a kind of toned-down version. I'm sorry to upset you, Peter. I'll leave now. I want to scout about the camp a bit. I'll see you tonight before the ceremony. Till then, you think about what I've said, okay?" Metellus left without giving Peter a chance to respond.

Peter did give the matter some thought, though nothing he could think of persuaded him to change his mind. He had too much invested in the thing now. And what harm could come of it? Metellus seemed to have survived it with no difficulty. And what was he worried about all of a sudden? It was dark in the hut, and, while not quite as hot as in the countryside below, the place was still pretty sweltering. So Peter did what he often did on such days. Without actually deciding to, he slept.

He dreamed. In his dream, Metellus returned earlier than he had said he would. He had a sense of great urgency about him, said he had managed to remember something. But the more he pleaded with Peter to get up and leave the compound with him, the deeper Peter seemed to sink into slumber. It was a strange dream, and Peter began to forget it as soon as he felt hands shake him awake. They were black hands, Metellus's he thought at first, but no. The priest had sent him the two unspeaking escorts as he had promised. Peter was happy to join them and surprised, once the door opened, to see that it was already dusk. And no sign of Metellus. Well, probably he was on his way to the ritual area where the crowd was beginning to reassemble.

Metellus, too, he remembered, was due to undergo an initiation this night.

Smiling faces greeted the outsider, about to become an insider. The throng parted like a curtain to let him penetrate to the center, where the old priest, in ceremonial finery, stood holding a ceramic cup. He was already chanting. It did not sound like Creole. The postulant met the old man's glance, smiling and, he hoped, reverent. But he could not help stealing a glance here and there to check on Metellus's presence. Still he did not appear.

Peter was made uneasy by the strange language, filled with gutturals and grunts, yet also with tongue-twisting, liquid-sounding accents, almost melodious, and yet somehow bestial. It became clear, as the priest neared a crescendo, that he was reciting the conditions of an oath, the Oath to Damballah. Peter knew he should shortly have to assent to whatever it was they were requiring of him. If only Metellus were here to help him make some sense of it all. But then, he thought ruefully, he was the anthropologist! He should be able to figure it out. Well, there was nothing for it now but to go on with the drama. When the priest stopped, looking expectantly at Peter, the latter nodded and bowed, hoping that would suffice. It must have, for the old man said something else unintelligible to his congregation, and they broke into wild applause and joyful shouting. Women and children came forth to place flower wreathes around his neck, a laurel wreath upon his sweating brow. Several dipped their fingers in the cup the old priest held, then made crosses on Peter's face and forehead with the red substance contained in the cup. After all had their chance, the old man offered the cup to Peter and bade him, this time in clear Creole, to take a drink. Peter knew by now that it must be sacrificial blood. But he was not one to be shocked or disgusted at alien mores, much less alien diet. As a field anthropologist, he could never afford such scruples. So he took the cup and drank of the salty beverage. More cheering followed. He guessed he had successfully taken the First Oath of Damballah. Now he need only wait to discover what secrets the initiation entitled him to. It was a cross-cultural constant: initiates into any cult received catechism about the inner truths, though still deeper secrets might well remain pending further degrees of initiation, degrees he dearly hoped might not take him too long to attain. It was all a matter of research, and of making friends with these people. And that shouldn't be too hard. Like all Haitians he had met, they were plainly good-natured and friendly.

The drums began to throb, and his pulses involuntarily picked up the pace. The priest gestured toward one of the huts, and Peter realized the ritual was not over after all. He looked at his initiator, then in the direction he had pointed. Shrugging, he decided he was game, and started for the hut. Now he noticed the drummers were moving into a circle around the small structure. As the shaman walked

beside him, Peter ventured to whisper to him, "Grandfather, you do me great honor. But where is my friend? Was not he, too, to receive initiation tonight?"

The oldster smiled and bobbed his head enthusiastically. "So he was. And so he did, less than an hour ago. You will see him soon enough. And now, my son, you will learn the secrets of life and death. First life. The Second Oath of Damballah." So saying, he pushed open the flimsy door. Peter went through it and gazed around the close quarters. There was room for a pad on the ground, and it was not unoccupied. Her black flesh gleaming in the light of banks of candles, the very incarnation of Haitian female vitality stretched out invitingly. His pulses hammered, his hormones surging. The drums outside did his thinking for him, though thinking had little to do with a situation like this! She was naked, and in a moment, he was, too. As he mounted her, as impatient as she of preliminaries, he got a good look at her face and saw two things with a gasp. He recognized her as the woman at whose cottage they had left Metellus's car. And her eyes were completely vacant, whites showing, lost in a rapture that was at least as spiritual as sexual, probably more. Peter understood that she was in the midst of a possession trance, no doubt believing herself to be indwelt by the spirit of the love-*loa* Erzulie. He had never imagined making love to a woman in such a state. As he entered her, pumping madly, he found she was like a volcano, a bucking mustang. It was all he could do to hold on, to gain purchase and drive himself home again and again till explosive release came. It was glorious!

He was winded, rolled over, felt her lithe limbs shuddering, shivering, coming to a gradual relaxation. Still she said nothing. And in the post-coital silence Peter could detect the low tones of an antiphonal chant. On one side of the hut, he could make out male voices. They repeated an invocation, *Nigguratl!* Then the female voices responded, *Yig!* He wondered what it meant specifically. He knew what it meant generally: he had just participated in a holy rite older than Baal and Asherah, the *Hieros Gamos*, or sacred marriage between god and goddess, between heaven and earth. It was supposed to be a magical guarantee of fertility for the fields. As this went through his mind, he realized for the first time he had exposed his piebald, half-dyed flesh! But the woman had been past noticing.

He had barely managed to wipe himself down and replace his clothes when the old priest swept the door open, exposing him to the laughing, eager faces of as many of the cultists as could get a view inside. The old man beckoned him to come out, while a couple of older women rushed past him to see to the woman, who was beginning to rouse from her trance. He was still reeling with ecstasy and exhaustion, but there was evidently to be no break. Eager hands ushered him into a smaller hut, this one with smoke ebbing from the door corners. He dimly observed that it was no doubt a sweat lodge, part of the universal pattern of the rites of passage. You could find them in preliterate cultures the world over: Amerindians, Siberians, Melanesians, Amazonian Rain Forest dwellers. All of them did it. In Peter's preconscious mind rested the knowledge that the smoke hut symbolized the womb of the second birth, birth unto a higher plane. It would be an ordeal, designed, through oxygen starvation and sensory deprivation, to produce visions, usually visions mirroring the traditional totem-masks of the tribe. What would he see, if anything?

Half-stumbling, partly due to the shoving of his escort, partly to his residual light-headedness, Peter fell to the ground inside the fire-lit hut. The ground was plain but not hard. The light flickered with its source. He felt a great urge to surrender to sleep. When had he slept so much? He could not remember. He drifted, drifted. He supposed he was asleep again, because now there appeared to be a row of figures stooping and sitting before him, too long a line for the small space to accommodate. He thought that he ought to know them. There was surely something familiar about them. And then he remembered he had marked their faces the previous night, at that ceremony he had largely forgotten. Maybe he would remember more of it now that they were here again, the *bocors*, the *houngans*, the tattooed and branded sorcerers of the cult. The firelight did strange things to their outlines, that was for sure, but it seemed to Peter that it was their shadows that were strangest of all. They did not seem remotely to correspond with the bodies casting them. The man in the middle, with the hoop ear rings and the worst scars along his neck: the shadow that loomed above him reminded Peter vaguely of the outlines of Great *Tulu*, the pincers attached to rolling necks and appendages. The others were all different but equally ill-fitting. Yes, the Old Ones . . . He was beginning to remember . . .

The spokesman for the group opened his eyes, and Peter saw no iris or pupil, only an empty expanse of glowing green, as when a ray of sunlight penetrates the sea water above a diver. The figure started to speak. It seemed as if he had been speaking for some time, as if someone had turned on a radio in the middle of a speech. But the content was definitely directed to him. "We know it is knowledge that you seek. The true seekers come to us sooner or later, as you have come. Here they learn the higher path, the path to the past. Which can come again. But you are special, Young Sir. The Old Ones have sent you to us for a purpose. You can help us to bring back the past of the Old Ones."

Peter felt he should be sitting in a posture of respect or veneration to these old saints, these elders of the community. But he was utterly empty, barely able to grasp what was being said. He lay there like a limp doll, hoping they would take no offense.

"We know you want to learn our secrets so you may gain fame by betraying them to the outside world. That you cannot do. But you will gain your fame. You will write your book. We will tell you what you may say. Others will even be able to verify what you say. And when you have your fame, we will have it. And then we will send one to you with something else you may tell your world. It is a world that loves the drugs. Substances." A ripple of laughter followed this.

"In that day, maybe two, three years down the road, when you are the so-famous professor, you will tell them you have discovered something great among us. You will tell them the old island witch-doctors are not so stupid. That they have chemical secrets from the rain forests. Powders that can lift the spirit, that can extend the manhood, that will shrink the fat from the white man's ass. And it will. And it will do other things their tests will not show. And in this way, you, my son, will open their hearts to love the past of the Old Ones. And in that day you white men will sing as we sing: 'That is not dead which can eternal lie. And with strange eons, even death may die!'"

He didn't see them leave. Maybe he had blacked out, lost consciousness even within the dream. But at length he roused again, sure by this time that he had been secretly drugged, even before being brought here to the sweat lodge. Now the fumes were making him cough. That's it — he had coughed himself awake. There was something in the smoke that was playing hell with his sinuses, that kept him confused, too. But that, of course, was part of the regimen. It didn't worry him unduly. But it entered his head to wonder about Metellus. Was he elsewhere in the camp, undergoing something similar?

And then: there he was! Peter flinched with shock, as welcome as the sight of him was.

"Peter! I made a big mistake bringing you here!" The image of his friend hovered nearby. The man must be kneeling to look into Peter's sodden face. Peter smiled and reached out to touch the other's shoulder in reassurance, but he could not reach him somehow.

"No, no, Met. It's all going well! Better than I could have . . . Say, that's quite a scar you've got there . . . How'd you . . ."

The black visage, curiously dim and gray in the smoky interior of the hut, waited for Peter to compose himself, to get his thoughts straight.

"Hear you passed your initiation rite, or test, or . . . Give me a minute . . ."

"Yes, *mon ami*, I took the Third Oath of Damballah, all right. With the Third Oath one renders oneself entirely to the Old Ones."

"Well, I can tell you, buddy, the Second Oath's not s'bad! I never had such a . . ."

"What about the First Oath, my friend? Did you taste the drink? The salty cup?"

"Yes, it was blood, I know. I knew it would be. Very common in these things. Probably one of their goats."

FROM THE PITS OF ELDER BLASPHEMY

"I think it was a goat named Metellus," the black man said, closing the mouth in this face and opening the new lips of his throat into a horrible grin. "It is no mere scar. You now have my blood in you. That is why I may come to you in this manner, while your mind has been opened to the influences. I have little time left. You have little time left."

Peter was shaking himself awake, shruggingly gathering himself into a sitting position. His wide eyes looked on the face of his dead friend, and the greater his sobered clarity became, the dimmer the features of Metellus became. "No, Metellus, I . . ."

The words came as a sourceless whisper: "You dare not leave and disobey the Old Ones now. They will not permit it. Do not openly defy them. But do not serve them. I will . . ." And there was no more. But Peter was now very definitely awake. His head pounded without benefit of drums. The smoke was about dispersed, which, he figured, was probably what allowed his head to clear. He lay down for a second, found that this only made his head hurt worse. So he rolled over to kneel and stand, but as he rolled, he encountered a supine form and recoiled. At first, his memories mixed up, he imagined it was the woman from a few hours before. But it wasn't.

He sprang backwards away from the machete-butchered carcass of Metellus. It hadn't been just his throat. That must have been only the beginning. He hadn't looked like this in the dream Peter had just awakened from. But he could no longer begin to guess, in this place, what was a dream and what was waking reality, or even what the difference was supposed to be. Anything was equally real, it seemed.

He flung open the fragile door and staggered out. A semicircle of the cult elders, a couple of their musclemen, and a few little boys awaited him. His dramatic appearance caught some by surprise, awakened others. The little fellows scattered, their interest in the stranger at an end for the time being. The others, rising to meet him, seemed subtly to come too close, their chests hoisted as if to signal threat, forming a cordon around him. A strange way to treat a guest and a new brother in the faith! But they must have a pretty good idea what was going through his mind. Mustn't he be weighing his old loyalties against his new ones? He would in a short time seal off the past and identify fully with the cult. That would be easier, of course, the longer they could keep him here among themselves, isolated from his professional colleagues and family members back home.

He met their polite questions as to his welfare with equally empty answers. He knew he was meant to see the corpse of Metellus. It must somehow be part of the ritual experience, "the secrets of life and death." It also no doubt stood for a warning that the same thing could happen to him should he have second thoughts. Peter thought better

of expressing his sorrow and rage at the ritual murder of his friend. It could only increase their suspicion. Better for the moment to let them think, as they no doubt did, that as a white man (oh yes, they knew all right: "you white men"), he regarded Metellus merely as an expendable hireling.

"I . . . saw great things. Heard great words. Words of destiny . . ." The older men smiled and looked at one another. He knew they had been waiting to hear something like this.

During the long afternoon, Peter listened and took extensive shorthand notes as the oldest of the cult elders fulfilled the promise made to him, that initiation should carry the privilege of disclosure. He got an earful of the lore of the cult. There was very little about the history of the group. Life changed very little in their tiny world from year to year, even from century to century, with the exception of the disruption of slavery. But the faith could go on and did go on, with only the temporary lack of sacrifices, in the slave quarters. And occasionally they had been able to get to the swamps on certain nights. By far most of their lore concerned the Old Ones, old gods, as he already knew, but now he sat entranced with morbid fascination at tall tales and weird theogonies unlike any he had encountered in his wide study of folklore and mythology. It was a treasure trove, and a genuine ancient tradition. There was far more here than he had dreamed of when he first dared hope there might exist in remote Haiti an untapped trove.

Most of what they told him, he was made to understand, he would be permitted to communicate to the outside world in the form of scholarly monographs. It was a sacrifice of traditional secrecy, to be sure, but even that was necessary to pave the way for the past of the Old Ones to come again. All men must know their Masters so that they might render them a fitting welcome when the great day came. Peter understood that there were yet greater arcana to which his two degrees of initiation did not yet entitle him, and of these he dared not ask, nor were the elders likely to permit them to be spread abroad.

Nor was Peter especially eager to advance farther along on the cult's path of discipleship, given what he knew had happened to poor Metellus at the climax of his initiation. He kept thinking of those last words his friend's shade had uttered in the dream vision. He had left him a dilemma, a riddle. He dared not give any sign of resisting or renouncing his role in their insane conspiracy, yet neither could he afford to become their accomplice, really their puppet, in it. He waited, as if for a signal he knew could never come: a signal from a dead man.

The catechism went on for days and then weeks. He could hardly imagine there was so much to the religion! It must be ancient indeed for the legendry to have become so complex, so fulsome, so baroque! There was no way of knowing how old the belief was. Their own lore said that it went back, of course, to the Old Ones themselves, and that

they had come to this planet from somewhere else entirely. But here history had shaded off into mythology. The true story would never be known. Peter found he was beginning to think like an anthropologist again. He found himself, as he looked over his notes by firelight each evening, musing over possible methodologies to make sense of the seemingly confused symbols and myths. He felt even Levi-Strauss would find himself outwitted by these old myth-mongers! Well, one thing anyway: if he managed to get out of here alive and unharmed, he had more than enough for a monograph, no, a series of them that would make Victor Turner's famous studies of the Ndembu look like a kid's description of a birthday party!

If only he could leave it at that. But a dark pall hung over him. There was little chance, he now realized, that they would hinder his return to the outer world (he once would have called it "the real world," but who knew what that was anymore?). Indeed, his role in their plan depended on that. But how many more atrocities must he be implicated in before he left? Back home, he could put that part of it out of his mind. Cultural relativism and all: who was he, a Westerner, to judge their ancient customs? And so on. But there was a ritual tonight in which the Old Ones would be invoked, and believers would receive their expected foretaste of the ecstasy of the past of the Old Ones, a past which now looked closer than ever to returning, thanks to their new brother. He knew he could not stand seeing any more of the poor wretches picked out of the crowd to die in a bloody holocaust as part of the ritual. Yes, he now remembered all too well what had transpired on that first night.

He had a seat of honor alongside the ranks of shamans and *bocors* inside the circle. Behind him gathered a number of children, whom he hated to contemplate seeing what he feared they would see, though he knew they must be hardened to it by now. Peter was a favorite of the children, especially as his skin, free of the dye, had begun to lighten and lighten, until it approached very nearly its original hue. This fascinated the children, who followed him around like baby ducks.

The time came, and soon, as he feared, one of the priests began to intone the familiar invocations. He was interested to note that, even though they no longer had to be judicious in the presence of outsiders, the crowed persisted in the ancient formula, calling on the names of the *vodun* deities that masked the terrible entities they actually served. He knew that traditions endure even absent their original rationale. So here came the names: Legba, Ogoun, Erzulie, Damballah, Samedhi . . .

As before, the crowd's enthusiasm was pent and building. But suddenly something surprised them. Something was going on at the rear of the circle. Peter craned his neck, trying to see over the shoulders of the old men. In a moment he could tell that the same thing, whatever it was, was going on all around the outer perimeter. Instinctively, he turned to his young entourage, gathered behind him, and sternly told them in his clearest Creole to get out, go to their homes, even out of the village, now.

The commotion was building. He could hear numerous physical impacts — bodies falling? Crowds clashing in battle? Was a riot beginning? Were some already intoxicated? Screaming began, and not just screams of alarm or of pain. There were shrieks of holy terror that ripped through the cotton humidity of the jungle night. Peter was on his feet, moving around aimlessly, uncertain what to do. If it was a fight, what side should he be on? How could a company of men approach the compound undetected? He began to slip on skids of blood on the packed ground, then to trip over bodies. A bloody harvest was progressing with amazing speed. He guessed that he, too, would momentarily fall under the scythe. Lanterns swung wildly and were extinguished. Torches bobbed and some went out. Some were swung as weapons, but ineffectively.

Suddenly, in the midst of the melee, Peter was sure that his sweat-stinging eyes glimpsed the impossible visage of Metellus, his livid gash gaping. But the gross wound did nothing to impede his prowess with the machete. He hacked and hacked without the fatigue of the living. Dead, he had himself become the Grim Reaper. But he did not fight alone. Like a gang of laborers chopping down jungle growth to clear a field or the path for a road, there was a whole crew of forms wielding knives, clubs, machetes. All silent. None of their faces was visible given the bad lighting. But the nearest one seemed incongruously to be sporting a top hat and sun glasses over a gaunt form one would not have thought sturdy enough to inflict the blows he was dealing.

The *bocors* and cult priests, taken by surprise, began to rally. They had no earthly weapons, but Peter could see their hands and arms flailing as if they bore deadly cudgel and sword. He knew they must be conjuring. It looked like superstitious pantomime, but Peter could tell something was happening because of what he heard, or thought he heard. He seemed to catch the echoes of explosions without the explosions themselves. Aftershocks of invisible eruptions. Something was occurring on a plane he could not see. But whatever it was, it had little effect on the invaders. One or two seemed to vanish, not to fall smitten, but just to disappear. But then perhaps they were leaving of their own accord now that the massacre was near its end. In the hacking fury of Metellus's vengeance, with the aid of

his mysterious hosts, tattooed heads flew like coconuts in a windstorm. Blood rained down, and Peter found himself spitting it out as he could not prevent a good bit of it entering his nose and mouth. Indeed, there seemed a red fog which made him gag and cough till he thought his lungs would burst.

He made for the edge of the clearing, where he could see the terrified yet curious young faces following the whole ghastly business. Their eyes grew even wider, if possible, as he approached, a wild and terrifying sight, he knew. But once he was upon them, and they kept looking past him, he knew another was the object of their gaze, and he turned to face it. It was Metellus. He gave a look to his dripping machete and cast it away, into the trees. He extended an arm toward Peter, but when the latter made a move to join him, Metellus waved him off. He tried to say something, but there was no sound, and Peter could not read his lips. He knew it was a final parting gesture, though. And then there was no one.

Peter's ears felt the pressure of sudden and total silence. None of the adults could have survived. But neither were their conquerors anywhere to be seen. Yet he knew where they were: wherever Metellus was. The true *loa* had taken their revenge, and Metellus had shared in it. As for him, Peter knew what he must do next. He would round up the newly orphaned children of the village and, with them in tow, begin the long journey back down the mountainside to the cottage. A few could return with him to town in the Jeep; the rest could be picked up by the authorities. He hoped they could all find homes, and anything would have to be an improvement.

He paused for a moment, looking in the direction of his hut. His papers and notes were there, even a tape recording or two. His book, yet unwritten, was there. His career was there. But now who would believe any of it? The myths and rituals of a small community — now all dead in a massacre? A massacre he alone had survived? How would any of that look? He turned his back on the village, counted the children, and started for the foot path.

Surely Hugh B. Cave needs little introduction to fans of weird fiction. Author of more than 700 short stories (as well as dozens of books), he was one of the grand old men of horror fiction. This story is one of his last works. He last appeared in Strange Tales *in the January 1933 issue.*

BY HUGH B. CAVE

HELLO MY RAG TIME GAL

by Friday Jones

Kinsella knew almost from the first cut that this was not the one. But still he had to make sure. He had to get his hands on her, part her, look inside and rub the fluids of her between thumb and forefinger under his nose before he could be sure.

She was not the one.

He left her cooling, the smell of her unwashed flesh fading with the heat of her body as he went cursing into the London fog.

Still, he consoled himself, if necessary practice would make perfect.

Anthony Lyons and Clay Kinsella had found their mutual interests when their hands met on the key to the locked cabinet in the boarding school library. They had both studied the habits of the head librarian and the locking and unlocking of the various doors, and had chosen the exact same time to try to get a copy of a book which was rumored to be in that cabinet; a book the title of which might have been been pronounced *J'KThr-rph*. Soon afterwards, their alliance would be sealed in blood, as they bent over chairs side-by-side to get their caning from the Headmaster.

Out of school, they joined their forces and fortunes to start along the Path, using forbidden tomes and deliberately forgotten scraps of knowledge to seek, to strive, to question, to raise up and to cast down. They purchased a ratty warehouse in Whitechapel, carefully camouflaged it to the casual eye, and then raised up their concealed Circle. Their research proceeded apace; the sewers under the warehouse bore more and more dubious offerings to the Thames River, while their journals and notebooks swelled like poisonous mushrooms growing on a grave.

More and more often, it was Kinsella who suggested the daring, the impulsive, the long-reaching — whereas Lyons was always in favor of holding back, double-testing each ingredient and incantation and avoiding anything too tentatively documented in the past — after all, only successfully completed spells got recorded, because failure usually meant death.

Kinsella would accuse Lyons of taking three steps backward to avoid taking one forward; Lyons would retort with the colorful tale of how his own headstrong mage-father had been found twisted into a ropelike strand of muscle and blood, threaded through a rathole in his study. But it was Kinsella's studies of a decidedly worm-eaten copy of his grandfather's grimoire which had suggested the possibilities of something much more powerful that could be called by them both, and made to stay and serve.

There were hints in several tomes, jotted notes in margins of books separated by continents and centuries, that when all combined told of how a creature with one foot on this plane and one in the next could be tempted to dream on this plane, supping the savors of the world through its host's eyes even while a mantle of spells was woven around it. The crude woodblock print that Lyons found loose in the back of a portfolio did not look too impressive — until you realized that the round, froggish-looking creature was clutching a fully-grown bull in one oddly-fingered "hand."

Although Lyons at first was hesitant, citing the many cautionary tales of what could go wrong in the calling and the feeding, soon he was swept up in his partner's fever.

The ritual would need five potential hosts. Corrupt hosts, fallen women whose shameful pleasures would be an irresistible lure to the thing from Outside. The chosen woman would be 'pregnant' with the thing most easily named a *g'rng* for ten months; seven of those months would resemble a normal pregnancy, and the last three would most definitely not. The *g'rng* would emerge from its dreaming, a creature fully fed of this plane, a powerful tool to be used in Magick of the darkest kinds.

Lyons was fascinated by the possibility of taming and training the demon, using its nonhuman throat to speak certain spells that no human mouth could pronounce. It was said that the voice of the *g'rng* was pleasing to the ears — or whatever — of the Outer Gods, and Lyons had fantastically ambitious visions of luring Them from where They danced.

Kinsella had other ideas, and he argued with Lyons about it as they scrubbed themselves with salt water after a preliminary ritual to properly cense their Circle.

"Look at the world!" he said, angrily laving flakes of blood from his hair. "It is changing like the seasons. Philosophy, government, religion, machinery — everything is evolving faster than the mind can hold. We are on the verge of a great new era — and I would live to see it! And rule it! There are spells in my grandfather's grimoire that can fuse a man's flesh with that of the g'rng, fill him with its strength and power. We could both sleep and dream the centuries away and then emerge!"

Lyons shook his head as he daintily cleaned the corners

of his eyes with the water, despite its salty sting. "And the g'rng would feed upon us like a leech that sucks flesh and bone and soul! When we awoke, we would be nothing but a dream that the g'rng would soon forget. Do you want to spend decades wrestling to keep your mind sane and whole in the embrace of a demon? And the longer the sleep, the deeper the feast that ends it. No, Clay, I forbid it. Once it is bound to us, we will study it and then decide."

Kinsella was silent, as he carefully picked strands of cat's-hair from between his teeth. And silently, he reminded himself to look up certain phrases in his grandfather's grimoire — and memorize them . . .

For a ritual so powerful it did not look like it would take much time at all. As Lyons put it, either they finished it fast or it finished them faster. Five women, harlots only one step above rag-pickers, were drawn into the night fog . . . walking unseeing and unseen to the warehouse, to be shriven with a fragrant oil and sent into the Circle.

Lyons and Kinsella were outside the Circle for this ritual; if what they called could not be lured into sleep, it might well rage — and they would have offerings to distract it.

"What if one of these bauds is already with child?" asked Kinsella.

"All the better. The g'rng will have something to eat while it dreams," replied Lyons. He raised his hands, heavy with misshapen and peculiar jewelry, in a gesture of greeting — or embracing. Kinsella followed the gesture with one of his own, and repeated the bleatting, harsh words where the Book said it was necessary. He itched to try some of his own formulae — but restrained himself.

There was a sudden green rippling inside the Circle, as though the thinnest sheer silk had been drawn through the air. A long, slow peal of sound that might have been music or moan. The women dreamily and simultaneously made that tiny, indefinable sound in the back of their throats that a woman makes when she is penetrated. Then the light folded itself away and — it was gone.

Lyons made a cutting gesture with both hands and was already drawing the women outside of the Circle with his words — they came drifting towards him like so many drugged sheep, any spirit they may have had polished away by the force of their captors' occult-strengthened will. Kinsella frowned. "That's it?"

"That's it." Lyons looked smug as could be, and in a moment Kinsella could see why. The women had a — gleam — to them. It was faint, some-

thing to be seen out of the corner of the eye, and probably only a magician's eye at that, but the tiny shining was the same green as the one that had wavered inside the Circle.

Lyons continued, "In seven months, we call them back and find which one is carrying the g'rng. Even if one of them dies, the creature will live long enough in the grave for us to retrieve it. Then we will plan further."

Lyons addressed the women. "Go now, and forget!"

Kinsella kept his thoughts to himself. Now that the g'rng was here, and lost in its dream, perhaps he could take some action to remove it — and himself — from his too-timid partner's influences.

He had to be fast with the next one; just as she had come to his charming (literally) embrace and the kiss of his scalpel, a noise told him that he was not alone. But the first cut was enough this time; he could see that residual green glow vanishing the instant the mortal blow was struck. She was not the one.

He dropped her and dashed off into the fog, sliding between a trundling hansom cab and the dirty wall like a shadow. A glamour floated with him, turning all eyes away. The tiny, ephemeral glow that seemed to shine from the back of his eyes out was brightening; another one of them was close. Perhaps she was the Filled One. He would take his time with this one, and make sure.

When Kinsella returned from his latest night on the town, there was a surprise waiting for him.
Lyons was dead.
Definitely, horribly dead.
Kinsella stood outside the Circle and stared. Was this something that they had conjured up and incorrectly ban-

ished? Was there some shift, some break in the Patterns? Perhaps the g'rng had been freed from its dreams by Kinsella's hunt and come questing back for the ones that bound it? But he looked again at the ruins of his partner, and saw.

Lyons and Kinsella had always entered the Circle mother-naked, and each of them kept their hair and nails clipped unfashionably short. Every item within the Circle had been protected by spells, some of them generations old, to keep them from being manipulated by the Things they called up. Many a mage had accidentally forgotten to charm his censer or orb, only to have it smashed into his skull by invisible, hating hands!

But Lyons had made a simpler mistake. He had stripped and cleansed himself outside the Circle; he had stepped inside of it; and he had forgotten to take off his glasses.

Shards of glass and gold were embedded in the man's flesh, standing out in all directions like the quills of a ruffled hedgehog. His clotting blood on the floor was painted into a fantastic frenzy of runes that matched the ones carved into his flesh. Whatever had been waiting in the Circle had obviously divided Lyon's glasses into the tiniest possible slivers so that it could use them all to cut him — all at once.

Kinsella looked long and carefully at the book — part journal, part spellsource, and part cookbook — that still stood massive on its stand. He could probably enter the Circle and claim it, at certain and perilous risk. But . . . for what he was going to do now, he would not need it. It was his own journals that he would be drawing on. And already he could see the signs that the demon inside was feeding; gnawing away at the flesh inside the Circle. With Lyons dead, and Kinsella's spells inside the Circle nullified (he gestured with two fingers and said five words to make this so), it would soon make inroads on the furnishings as well; leaving behind only a horribly scorched place in the center of an abandoned warehouse.

It's always the last one, Kinsella scowled to himself as he pressed the woman down on her bed, knee to her chest and hand over her mouth. If you're looking for the full bottle, you'll always pick up the four empty ones first.

As he bent his arm to one side to clear her throat for the knife, he paused, ignoring her muffled cries. Or was it that the g'rng had been transferring itself from host to host as they died under his hands? Had his actions prolonged his own chase?

No matter. There was nowhere it could go now. He cut.

The whore's throat was still showering the pillow when Kinsella held her down with one hand and stroked her open with the edge of the scalpel. Another slice through a clinging layer of fat and twitching muscle, baring her womb. Another cut — and he saw it!

He saw a twisted flattened foot like a frog's. He saw the foot, as it vanished through a hole swiftly clawed into the

back wall of the womb, as the g'rng escaped into its host's entrails.

What happened after that took a long time — a long, long time. Kinsella had to carefully slice and peer through the woman's flesh, palpating each organ as he removed it to make sure the creature was not hiding there. The g'rng was as at home swimming in the woman's dying flesh as it had been dreaming in her womb. It hid in the partings of her cirrhotic liver; it leaped in and out of her spongy lungs until Kinsella pressed them flat between his fingers; it burrowed within her viscera (Kinsella was glad that it had not the wit to throw things; working with her pulpy waste oozing up all over him was bad enough); at the last extremity it chewed its way up through the base of the brain and hid in the woman's skull, and Kinsella had to hammer his shoe-heel against the scalpel driven into a facial fissure before he could pry a door into that cavern.

Finally it was in the light, cowering against the bared and scraped spinal column in the hollow of her chest.

Kinsella held out his hand and intoned, "Krnnbllo!"

The g'rng quivered.

"Krnnbllo! K'nhk gn'oo akko!" Kinsella said again, hoping that he was right, that after all of this work and blood it would know — and come.

Slowly, the little green homunculus crept out of the woman's chest. Kinsella held his hand palm out; and it reached up, fastening toes and teeth and tongue into his hand. Kinsella only smiled as it curled itself against the slight concavity of his bloodied hand and began to suck. He cupped his fingers loosely — oh so tenderly! — over his tiny prize, and went to the door. His heavy coat would cover his ruined clothing, and the walk was not a long one. Kinsella did not even look back at the steaming pile that had once been a woman.

Getting off his clothes with only one hand free was a bother, but it was necessary; he cut through his braces with his knife before discarding them. Naked in the fog, he carefully felt his way through the construction site.

Here.

The heavy stone slabs were waiting to be set into the walls of the dirt hole and form the foundation; the soil behind them was tight-packed, but Kinsella clawed methodically at it with a small mattock and finally his fingers, ignoring the snapped nails and bruises, until there was a downward-slanting, narrow hole — one that could hold a moderate-sized child. Or a man, if that man was to wedge himself into that hole, packing himself into it feet-first until his knees were tight to his sides and his arched back left only scant inches between his stomach and the dirt; until only one arm was free to gather up earth and rake it towards him, over his head and shoulders, burying his face and the scalpel clenched in his teeth.

Now his entire world was the tiny pocket of earth where

he lay curled, face down and intent, starting at the faint not-glow that seemed to come from his demon-nursing hand.

As he took the scalpel in the ruins of his free hand and reached down to slide the tip into his belly, just above the pubes, he felt no pain. No pain as he forced back a massive flap of skin, then slid the tiny form and his own hand into his body. The warmth of his intestines felt good on his chilled fingers, and the creature seemed to wriggle with pleasure as the heavy moist weight bulged over it. He flashed on a sudden image of Napoleon with his hand buried in his coat.

As the blood slowly pooled under him, he spoke the spell that he had carefully researched and memorized before his hunt had begun. It was a paean of ancient, terrible words that shuddered against his lips. Rippling lines of Power danced over and around him. He called on the demon to embrace his flesh, to absorb and enlarge it, to drink of the earth and of the strength of the people and the city around it until the day came when it would find itself free, gorged with power in a world without God. Woven into the spell like a poison snake through a child's fingers were words of strengthening of mind, of the g'rng submitting its will to him, the dominion of brain over body. As the chant faded with his strength, he felt the first tug of the alien mind against his, and set himself, braced back on his mental heels as it were, prepared for a dreaming of endless combat . . .

In the morning, the cursing workers shored up the dirt with a board before tilting the foundation stone into place. The blood-soaked clothes went unnoticed, trodden down into the soupy mud by hobnailed boots.

In the year 2038 demolition was not a process of smashing and rending stone and steel; it was infesting a building with a computer-controlled layering of microscopic machines, that would scan and disassemble the building down to its components. You would shake a bucket of nannites over a building and return the next day to find a pile of boards, or a pile of ingots and chemical containers, or a pile of dust if you preferred.

A deconstruction worker went over a building, made sure that the nannites had properly infested it, and monitored their work via computer as they ripped the building apart — and, in this case, put it back together again. It was a minor building from the late 1800's, but instead of being demolished, the building was to be rendered. The nannites would go through and scan the building, then carefully digest the inconstant wood and stone and replace them with spun-carbon foam and slabs that would be harder than diamond but capable of shifting like a boat under sail to ride out temblors. That was necessary; the building's foundation was becoming spongy with time, settling unevenly.

Yesterday, Soren Swann had gotten the ends of his dreads decorated with metallic beads which constantly sought each other, clicking together and apart in a tiny magnetic melody around his head. He was just checking that the nannites were all properly oriented, and had enough raw material to work with, when he turned to his partner and said, "What *is* that damn song you keep humming?"

"Dah-dah-da-dah-dah, dah-dah — oh that?" Joanne Reese smiled as she waved her sensor wand over the cornerstone. "Remember that cartoon, it's a real old one, about the guy who finds the frog in the foundation of a building?"

"No, I don't," said Soren, shortly.

"Yes you do! It's a singing frog, but it only sings when the guy's around, so he can't get it to perform on stage? It sings 'Hello my baby, hello my honey' — you remember that one!"

Joanne continued, as she started the ignition sequence of the nannites warming up. "Well, at the end of the cartoon there's a guy in the future, who's demolishing a building with a disintegration gun. And that guy finds the same frog, and runs off with it. I loved that cartoon as a kid."

Soren did remember the disintegrating building part anyway, but said nothing. He suspected that Joanne's singing was to cover up the clicking of his hair, which she had likened to the sounds of a deathwatch beetle chewing through a board.

Both Soren and Joanne checked their equipment for the last time, then started the nannites. The building seemed unchanged for the first minute; then, Soren pointed as the foundation lifted a quarter of an inch and then subsided. Joanne was looking at her enhanced-display screen, which showed the nannites frantically converting the roof and top story into more modern materials, while great plumes of waste heat jetted out of the windows.

The foundation heaved another quarter of an inch, then two inches, then it was out of the ground and blocks of stone were hanging in the air over the stunned workers. One block dropped slantwise across Joanne, crushing her to the pavement. Her head was pinned in the choking dust; she couldn't see; her free hand pounded red and futile at the ground and then relaxed as she died.

Soren was untouched as the stones fell around him, the building sliding *up* and *away*, rolling down over the pulsating sea-green bubble that seemed to have risen under it. Then the bubble raised one giant seven-fingered paw and smashed it onto the pavement, barely registering the tiny unevenness that was suddenly all that was left of Soren. It rose, or swelled, or otherwise brought itself above the line of the city.

The g'rng looked out upon its kingdom with three shining black-on-gold eyes. Those eyes drank in the flying machines, the soaring arches of buildings stretching off into the distance, and it would have smiled if it had lips.

Lightning flickered between those eyes, then about its head. It opened its mouth and sang a single discordant note . . .

And deep in the soul of every living creature who heard that note, something nameless and totally unnatural awakened. And began to dance.

Friday Jones is nobody's Gal Friday, but she has been a staunch ally of horror fandom for many years, creating and editing the unique and spunky fanzine Parts (dedicated to Lovecraft's Herbert West plus the Church of the Sub-Genius!), and putting in huge efforts and talents to help organize and run the NecronimiCon programs in the 1990s.

THE CAVE OF BAPHOMET

by Richard L. Tierney

From teeming Makkah's moiling market-place,
Unto Al-Ghar Al-Layat, Cave of Night,
Baphomet came in hopes to see the face
Of One Who offers gardens of delight
To all who in submission worship Him.
Therein he heard strange echos thrumming from
Far underground, as of a deep-toned drum,
And as he sat in prayer both night and day,
He seemed to hear as from vast gulfs below
In vibrant intonations dark and grim:
"I am your Lord. Submit thy will to me
"And thou shalt live in bliss eternally."
Then from the dark rose up a hulking shape,
Toadlike in form, with fearsome fiery eyes,
And from its throat there came in croaking tones
A message of malovelance and doom:
"I am Tsahog-'gallah, Lord of Old Night.,
"And unto you, my thrall, I say: Recite!
"Convey my runes of bale unto thy kin
"And lead them forth in zeal with fire and sword
"To scourge and conquer all the lands of earth."
Then Baphomet, amazed, obeyed his Lord
And spread the Message that would be the birth
Of conquests that would ravage all the lands
And glut in sacrifice the darksome soul
Of black Tsathag-'gallah, his Lord of all.

BEEN THERE, SEEN THAT . . .

by Charles Garofalo

Even when the doctor told him the news, Blaine couldn't believe it. He'd wanted to hear just that news for more than a year, but when it came, it was just too good for him to accept.

"This is on the level?" he demanded, trying not to sound like an excited brat. "My sight's . . . coming back?"

Dr. Morse was currently a dark gray form silhouetted against a lighter gray background. Sometimes Blaine could see him as a blurred human outline, sometimes he was just a dark blob. Still, he was seeing more than he'd seen since . . . it happened.

"It's the only thing it could be," Morse explained.

"But I thought that only happened in the movies," said Blaine, too afraid of disappointment to wholeheartedly accept it. "The guy gets blinded by a knock on the head, then another blow brings his sight back."

"No, it does happen, though not anywhere near as often as those scriptwriters make out," said the doctor. "What do you think gave the movie people that idea? How did you hit your head this morning, anyhow?"

"Kinda embarassed t' say, Doc," said Blaine. "I'm usually careful about it and can do my calesthenics without havin' any trouble. Today I miscalculated, though, and cracked my head against the wall doin' my sit-ups. I know, I shoulda' had someone watchin' me, but I can't always get somebody t' do that, and excercise became kinda an obsession for me after I was blinded. I didn't want t' just sit around and get fat and soft and become a total wreck."

Dr. Morse didn't have to know about his periodic over-indulgence in booze, and pot when he could get it, although he probably suspected it. It would belie Blaine's story about exercising for his health. Well, he did exercise for his health. Blaine kept himself as tough and muscular as he could manage with the calisthenics just in case anybody he'd crossed in the past heard about his blindness and decided to visit him and pay off old scores now that he was handicapped. A lot of people he knew *would* do something like that.

"It was lucky, and with long odds," Morse explained, "but it happened. Your eyesight should return gradually . . . you can already distinguish light and dark and can see solid objects. Of course, your eyes will be sensitive to light at first, and they may be weakened. Although I see no atrophication, mercifully. Of course, I'd strongly recommend you stop getting hit on the head, but there's other good reasons besides your eyesight for giving that up."

"There's one thing," said Blaine. "Since this morning, I've . . . been seein' things even with my eyes closed."

"What sort of things?"

"Well . . . they're blurred, but I think I see forms, and movement sometimes, like I do when my eyes are open. But it's like somethin' else is goin' on behind my lids if I close my eyes for any length of time. No details yet . . ."

"Don't worry, you're just getting used to light all over again. It's an after-image you see when you close your eyes, that's all. Now, you're going to have to see a specialist to be checked out, and start a whole new program of care and treatment, but I think you'll find it worth it . . ."

Blaine's eyesight got clearer daily; by the end of the week he could see, and though he was sensitive to light, in just a few weeks time he could read and see fine detail. His year of alternately begging God for a miracle and cursing Moriggi to hell and everything else he could imagine was over.

The only trouble was, he now could see the details when he closed his eyes as well.

The therapist Dr. Morse had sent Blaine to quickly diagnosed his new problem . . . and got it half right.

"You stay up too late," she told him. "I know, this has to be exciting for you, but staying up reading or watching TV isn't good for you."

"I . . ." sputtered Blaine, in a way that would've had the people who'd known him before the "accident" shaking their heads in disbelief. "I . . . it's like bein' a kid again, with Christmas every day. I try to sleep and I just can't. It's even worse than readin' or watchin' TV. I'm tired, I lie in bed, and I can't sleep. I just toss and turn a lot."

"If that keeps up, we might have to put you on a sleeping pill," the lady said. "But I don't want to do that just yet. You have enough problems right now without pills. You can get hooked on them so fast . . ."

Tell me about it, thought Blaine, whose perchant for booze and certain other diversions had gone back to well before his blindness. Of course, he didn't dare tell her or Dr. Morse about what was really keeping him up. It was too weird. He didn't want to end up at a psychiatrist's office. He wasn't nuts, but that sort of head-doctor might know enough about guilt and symbolism to figure out what he'd done. He didn't want to get his sight back just to spend the next twenty years or so looking out on a cell block.

The trouble was, when he closed his eyes, now, he kept

seeing. If he just blinked, or just closed them for a very short time, it was all right, but if he closed them for any length of time, he'd see *that place* again.

He'd grown familiar with that place during the weeks he regained his eyesight, when he'd had to rest his eyes for long periods because they were weak and sensitive. Even though he quickly learned he could get away simply by opening his eyes and seeing the real world again, the place still scared the crap out of him.

Blaine had at first tried to explore the strange city he saw when he closed his eyes. But he got more scared every time he went there. Everything about that town was nasty or unpleasant, it was too much like jail, which he'd been in, or maybe prison, which he'd been threatened with.

He'd always see into the same city, which moved before his eyes like he was there and wandering through it. It was always night there, no matter if it was daylight in the real world. Despite it being dark, except for the dim streetlights that showed the city at irregular intervals, he could see it was a dirty, messy place, like the worst of the slums. Grime coated the streets and the litter was all over, some of it pretty revolting stuff. Some of it was weird as well, stuff that nobody in his right mind would throw away. He saw money lying in the gutter a few times, and it was piles of crumpled up greenbacks, not loose change. Other times he'd seen jewelry, a fur piece, a cell phone that looked like it still worked, all sorts of swell junk like that. Blaine regretted he couldn't stop and pick those things up to bring home, though he was grateful he couldn't smell or feel anything in his visions, and that while he could hear, there was little *to* hear.

The buildings were uniformly ugly. They were all these big, dilapidated tenement buildings, which gave every indication that they'd been awful-looking when they'd been new, and had gotten worse with time. Some of them were completely dark, some had lit windows in them, but even the lit rooms didn't look inviting. Blaine couldn't see what was going on in any of them and didn't want to. All the tenements were tall buildings, almost tall enough to count as skyscrapers. In fact, they really did seem to touch the sky. Or rather the dark gray night sky, devoid of moon and stars, seemed low enough to rest on the buildings. If Blaine hadn't known better, he'd have thought the whole town had been built underground and the buildings were used to hold the big cavern's roof up like pillars.

The people he saw, and he saw a lot of them, were no more attractive than the buildings they lived in . . . or maybe, the way there was always a big crowd wandering aimlessly through the streets, they didn't like going inside the buildings either. Every one of them, man, woman and kid, was dressed like a bum, covered in baggy, ragged dirty clothes. The faces were all dirty and ugly as well, the faces of people who'd done time on the streets. Haggard, with glazed eyes, some disfigured by sores or acne, others by scars. The happiest people Blaine saw were the drunks and homeless people who'd crapped out on the sidewalk to sleep. Everybody else . . . didn't look well. Glazed eyes, vacant, zombie-like faces, some muttering, some staring out into space, some just looking angry and desperate. There wasn't one healthy or happy person in the crowd; they all looked like burnt out druggies, or crazy people living in their own worlds, or in some cases like they were fighting a bad illness.

There was something about this place . . . dreary. Worse than depressing, this place got you so down it was downright killing. Blaine had had to live in a slum for quite a while after leaving home, trying to get by on a shit job. He'd been in jail twice, once for working for a bookie, once for beating the crap out of a loudmouth while drunk. Neither jail nor the slums had been this . . . miserable. That was it, this place was just miserable, absolutely dead end. He'd thought jail had been bad enough: the cages, the boredom, and knowing what some of his fellow jailbirds might've done to him for fun if he hadn't been big and mean-looking. But he'd bet, given the chance, anybody here would've happily picked jail over this place. There was the air of hopelessness about it, something even he, who only saw into the place, didn't live there, might see. Like in one of those maxiumum security prisons, where the guys there knew they weren't going to ever get out, and where a breakout was impossible. Or some city in a poor country, which offered even less than the slums here did, where all you could expect was fifteen-sixteen hours a day hard work for pennies, with no prospects except starving in the gutter when you got too old to work.

The place was like one of those old factory cities, nothing but buildings as far as the eye could see. No trees or parks to break up the monontony, not even the vacant lot or the old foundation where a building had been torn down. Possibly there were roads out of this town, Blaine hadn't seen any of them. No doubt anybody who could get up the spirit to leave this place had left already. Weirder, Blaine didn't see any churches or missions, no soup kitchens, no place where anybody could deal out help and a sales pitch for their religion to the poor. That wasn't the way Blaine recalled the slums, there were always psalm singers and tract shufflers going down there to do good, especially since they knew lots of poor people grabbed the hope of heaven as an alternate to gambling, dope or booze.

He'd never seen a car or truck the whole time he'd been here either, not parked, not barreling though the streets scattering the milling pedestrians before it. Even most Third World cities had a fair amount of cars and trucks these days, even if they were all owned by the government or businesses! But nobody had even a bicycle here. Also, while he may just have missed it in his travels, wasn't any town or city supposed to have a waterfront? They needed a river or lake for drinking water.

BEEN THERE, SEEN THAT . . .

His travels? Blaine didn't go anywhere in the city, he just was along for the ride with somebody else. He was like a ghost who'd possessed someone else's body but couldn't control it. He couldn't feel, he could only look, with the same field of vision as if he was looking out of someone else's eyes, with no say as to where or when the guy turned his head and looked. He could see enough to know he was always with the same host, as he got glimpses of the same large, burly body, the same long brown coat, and the same raggedy work shoes every time the guy he was with happened to look down. No idea what the face looked like, and judging by the way the other people there looked, he didn't mind the fact he couldn't see it. The body seemed familar somehow, but he couldn't think of whose. He'd known more than a few big guys in his past, and was one himself. But he really thought he should know who he was with. Somehow, it scared him.

Shit, this whole place scared him. It really did. He hadn't liked it from his first clear look, and the more he saw of this town, the less he liked it. It didn't take more than few visits there to spook him.

Blaine couldn't even say why he was so spooked. All right, the place was miserable, but it didn't seem dangerous. He hadn't seen anybody pull a knife, throw a punch, or even look like they were going to do something so active. Everyone here seemed too whipped to think of taking out their frustrations on somebody else, even their own relatives or folks smaller than themselves. Since there were no cars, there were no bad drivers squashing unwary people. And while the weather seemed bleak and chilly, Blaine had never seen any sort of weather that could make people outside interrupt their treadmill routine: no blizzards, no water-freezing colds, no sweltering summer heat, not even any rain or thunderstorms. But the place got to him fast, made him force open his eyes in a hurry. The place itself scared him silly, something about the wiped-out, apathetic people there made him nervous, and he was even afraid of whoever he passed on the dingy, cracked sidewalks.

Finally, there was the Door. Blaine had no idea what the Door led to, it was just another fixture of the city. It was the most dreamlike part of his visits, the only genuinely freakish thing about his eerie adventure. The Door was never in the same spot in the city twice. Or perhaps there were a bunch of Doors all over that town. No, he'd pass through a familiar street a dozen times without seeing the Door, then spot it once, then it wouldn't be there the next time he and his partner went through there. He never got a good look at the Door. It was big, it was black, he thought it was metal, and there was a sign over it he never got close enough to read.

The sight of the Door was the one thing that could snap the local citizenry out of their apathy. The sight of it sent them backing away, visibly scared. His . . . host? . . . was as affected by the Door as anybody else, either doing a one-

BY CHARLES GAROFALO

45

eighty when he encountered it or walking by it on the other side of the street, as far away from it as he could possibly get. Everyone else acted the same way when they spotted the Door, like it might fly open any minute and the worst monster you could imagine would come charging out. Well, 'most everyone, anyhow. Twice Blaine had seen people go up to the Door, once a girl around eleven, wearing nothing but a snowsuit far too large for her, once a very tired-looking old man. He couldn't be sure if they got the Door open, because his host would always join the mad rush to get away when anybody tried the Door. He *thought* he saw the old guy get it open, but he couldn't be sure, and he definitely hadn't seen whether he'd gone in or something had come out.

The Door was another thing he was now afraid of. He hadn't been afraid of it at the beginning, but the locals' fear of it had communicated itself to him. Blaine now dreaded he might be around someday when the Door was opened and he couldn't get away, and he would see, and maybe experience, whatever happened. It didn't matter that all he needed to do to escape was open his eyes, or have his host make a getaway, Blaine was truly afraid sometime he wouldn't be able to manage it, just as he already dreaded a day when opening his eyes might not get him out of the miserable city.

That's why he'd been staying up late at night. He had to get himself so tired that he'd drop off in a hurry with no time to see into that place. All it took was a little look at that town and he was up all night. As it was, there wasn't any night now he slept that he didn't dream, but at least not every dream was a nightmare. Wherever he was visiting was a nightmare every time he visited it.

Blaine knew he needed to talk to somebody, somebody who was interested in dreams and shit like that, and might help him. But he didn't want to see a head doctor. A shrink might be a dumb quack who couldn't help him . . . or he might be smart enough to figure out what Blaine had done, and run to the police.

Well at least there was one obvious other choice. Problem was, Blaine had less faith in Silva than he had in psychiatrists. For cryin' all night, the guy kept fooling around with magic long past the point when he should've known better. The spells he recited for luck, the magic candles he burned to win the lottery, his trying to predict the future by astology, cards and a dozen other ways . . . but he still was working six days a week at that food warehouse to get his money.

Still, Silva at least was interested in dreams and visions and shit like that. And while he didn't especially like Blaine, he'd at least gone out of his way to do him favors after he'd been blinded, getting audio books and music for him out of the library. That was another weird thing about Silva, when he wasn't trying to be the next Anton LaVey he was always doing good works.

★   ★   ★

Silva, of course, was thrilled. Whatever experience had turned him into a believer in magic was long in the past, and Blaine's brush with the supernatural was here and now.

"And you never experience these visions with your eyes open?" he asked. "And never asleep, when you might dream it? Only when you close your eyes for more than a couple minutes?"

"I said that, didn't I?" growled Blaine testily.

Silva thought for a minute, then asked: "You don't think it could be your conscience speaking, do you?"

"What conscience?" Blaine snorted. "I don't have no conscience any more than you do."

"Well, your experience is the sort of thing that gets people thinking about their lives, and their past and future," Silva explained. "Regaining your sight like you did was pretty close to a miracle, and you might've started thinking about your past and wondering if what you've been doing with your life is right . . ."

"Look, I don't want to hear a sermon from a guy who tried to win a horserace by hexing the favorite! What's got you off on this morality kick anyhow?"

The would-be magician looked perfectly serious.

"Because," he explained, "the place your describing sounds a lot like hell. Literally."

"Hell?" said Blaine. "Oh, come off the crap! I'd recognize hell! There would've been fires, and devils runnin' around stickin' people in the ass with pitchforks, and . . ."

"That's how the Christians imagine hell," admitted Silva. "And the Buddists. But in the old Jewish manuscripts, and many of the older religions, hell wasn't a place of fire and brimstone. It was just a big, dark, dirty city where the spirits of the dead wandered around aimlessly, muttering to themselves like doped-up inmates of some psycho ward. They called it 'Sheol.'"

"But why do so many people make out hell to be a place of punishment?" asked Blaine. "I mean, it was rough, but hardly the torture chamber all those fundie Bible pushers make it out to be. It seemed better than what I've heard the big prisons are like, let alone a concentration camp or what you'd see in a war zone."

"You're forgetting one thing," said Silva. "If you live in the slums, you can hope to land a better job and move. If you're in prison, you can hope a smart lawyer'll get you a retrial, or you might serve your sentence. At any rate, you'd finally die in prison, so you're sentence would be over that way. Hell's *eternal*. No way out, no parole, and you've already died. Isn't being stuck in a place like you described forever enough punishment for most crimes? Maybe fire and brimstone might be suitable for somebody like a dictator who's caused incredible amounts of death and suffering, or a business tycoon who's screwed thousands of employees and millions of customers, but not for your standard everyday son-of-a-bitch like you or me."

"Shit," growled Blaine. "There's folks worse than either of us out on the street and God don't take time out from his busy schedule to warn them they're headin' for trouble. Not t' mention a helluva lotta people *better* than either of us who don't get this 'sinner repent' treatment either. Why should God suddenly decide to restore *my* sight, then make me see into hell?"

"They always say he's beyond human understandin'," said Silva. "Or maybe he thinks you're ripe for repentence, that he's got a chance of gettin' you into heaven if he works on you like this. My own feelin', I'll admit, is that it's in your head, not from God, that you've either got a guilty conscience about somethin', or the excitement of gettin' your sight back woke up some old fears and memories. Didn't you once tell me you were from a poor section of New York, just one step up from the slums?"

"Jersey City, but you got that right. My own neighborhood stunk, and just a few blocks over things got lots worse."

"Well, you might be subconciously remembering where you used to live. Can't help you much if it's that; I ain't no doctor or priest. If you don't like that idea, and don't like the idea it's your guardian angel warnin' you, I can't come up with any ideas . . . unless it was somethin' connected with the accident where you lost your sight orignally. You recall anything strange that happened when you had that accident, or just before? Something that'd make you think of hell or anything mystical? There's laws to magic that might've linked you to hell with the accident, if they work. At this point, even I ain't sure they do."

Blaine right now was forcing his feelings not to show on his face. There *had* been some details about the way he got blinded that would logically link his eyes to hell; even he, with no belief or understanding of magic, could see them. But he didn't dare tell Silva.

"What details?" he demanded. "I was fuckin' drunk! I fell down the stairs of my apartment and hit my head. I really wish I could forget that goddamn fall, but I can't. My two friends were at the bottom of the stairs, no one pushed me, I just lost my footing and fell. And when I came to, I couldn't see."

Silva had struck paydirt, though Blaine wouldn't give him the satisfaction of admitting it. Blaine could see well enough, now. And what he couldn't see, he *knew*. Knew it wasn't his conscience, that he was actually seeing into hell. Why else should the place spook him so, if it wasn't hell? The absolute dead end of the universe, the place you can't get out of, no matter what you do. Well, *he'd* gotten out of it . . . so far; he imagined some day he'd be a permanent resident there, but currently he could leave at will. More, he knew who he traveled with while he was down there. He ought to know. Moriggi, who had blinded him, and he had put Moriggi where he was now.

He didn't dare tell Silva that. But he did have a few questions more to ask.

"I occasionally see somebody unconcious in the streets down there," he mentioned. "If it were hell, how could anybody sleep or pass out? I thought you were supposed to be awake all the time down there."

"Who knows?" said Silva. "Maybe they were dummies put there to torment the others, seemingly free of hell for a few hours. Or maybe they were people who couldn't get into heaven, but had done enough good things durin' their lifetimes that their torment was lessened."

"But what about that soor?" asked Blaine, newly eager to hear what Silva might say. "Everybody seems afraid of a door that kept appearin' at odd places. Couple times I've seen people go through it. I've never seen them again, but I could easily have missed 'em. What could a door like that lead to? The fire-and-brimstone hell?"

Silva was silent for a minute. From the looks of him, it wasn't so much he didn't know what the Door symbolized, as that he did recognize the Door and didn't know how to put it to him.

"You didn't read many fairy tales as a kid, did you?" Silva asked suddenly. "Your mom didn't have a big book of 'em and read to you in bed?"

"A big collection with pictures from the Walt Disney movies in it," admitted Blaine. "But my Dad made her stop when I was six, said I was too old for it. Threw the book away, too, when I started readin' it myself."

"This wouldn't be in a Disney book," said Silva. "He never made a movie out of this story. Never even considered it. But before I say anything else, take a good look at that Door, see if it has any writin' on it, or over it. It could be real important."

"The guy I'm with avoids that Door like it's the entrance to a friggin' AIDS hostel! How am I supposed t' see what it's got written on it?"

"Try t' see, anyhow. It might be your way out of this if it is. Trust me. I'm afraid t' say more about it until you can tell me whether it is the Door I think it is or not."

Silva refused to say any more on the subject. Blaine managed to force himself not to try to pound the secret out of the pretentious idiot. Silva only got the bullshit he was spouting out of books. Blaine had real experience to go on.

And he already knew whose eyes he was seeing through down there. It could only be one person in hell he could be linked to like that.

Lou Moriggi. The man who'd blinded him more than a year ago.

The man he'd killed.

Blaine couldn't pretend he wasn't the one who'd killed Moriggi, even to himself. Yeah, Deuce and Fred had been with him, but he was the ringleader, and he was the one who'd really laid into that asshole with the hunk of pipe when he wouldn't hand over the money.

The three of them had come up with what had seemed like a foolproof racket. They'd found out that old man Johnson had been taking advantage of the job shortage by paying his workers cash under the table with no benefits or medical. Johnson's factory wasn't quite bad enough to be considered a sweatshop, and at the end of the week his workers left with better than a piddling sweatshop salary in their pockets.

Every payday, Blaine would lead Fred and Deuce, and they'd grab one of Johnson's boys on the way home from work, rough him up a bit, and rob him. They were careful not to hurt any of them too bad, just enough to let them know they meant business, and even made sure to nail a different guy every week, so they didn't completely bust somebody. Blaine and his boys had been bullies back in their school days, and they were really just using the old tactics. Only now they weren't just in it for milk money. The guys they mugged didn't dare complain to the cops. All of them were engaged in an illegal activity, some where illegal immigrants, and a couple were collecting unemployment or welfare besides their salaries. They didn't dare open their mouths. Neither did Johnson, who, despite his unethical business practices, was no gangster and couldn't just send muscle after the three of them. Blaine had been careful to watch just in case the factory workers compared grievances and decided to go after the three of them as a gang, but that had never happened. Okay, it was a real two-bit racket; it couldn't have supported the three of them by itself, but it guaranteed he and his buddies would have a real swell Saturday night.

Then that bastard Moriggi had turned the racket and Blaine's whole life to shit with his temper and attitude. They'd picked Moriggi for the target that last awful Friday night. They'd never tapped him for money before. The jerk apparently felt he was above being tapped for cash simply because he was a big, burly Italian with the lousy temper they were famous for. He had the nerve to tell the three of them fuck off (well actually Fred was coming up from behind him at that point, so it looked like it was only two of them), that he needed the money to pay his bills, and he'd worked hard for it. For Christ's sake, the guy hadn't just been asking for it, he'd been *begging* for it.

And they'd given it to him. Originally Blaine had just intended to teach the dumb son of a bitch a lesson, although he couldn't have spoken for his two buddies, but after Moriggi had managed to knock some of Fred's teeth out, and had landed a couple of surprising punches on Blaine, he'd lost it and gotten carried away, using the pipe to really work the guy over. It had gotten to the point where he'd actually been holding the creep up to beat on him with the pipe, while Fred and Deuce hung back and landed punches and kicks. It had seemed like every bit of the fight had been beaten out of Moriggi when . . .

The guy somehow got the strengh up to throw one last punch. It had really caught Blaine by surprise, that fist seeming to come out of nowhere and crash into his face. It had slammed right into his forehead, so hard Blaine heard Moriggi's fingers break when it had hit, despite feeling like he'd just caught a lightning bolt above the eyes. In spite of holding onto Moriggi he'd gone over backwards, cracking the back of his head good against the sidewalk.

He'd lucked out then. His pals hadn't gotten scared and run, like he'd suspected. First they'd got him back to his digs, then, realizing he'd had a major concussion, had called an ambulance, making up the story about his tumbling down the stairs and banging his head several times. Blaine still wondered why'd they'd done that; neither of his pals had actually seemed the kind who'd really stick their necks out for him. Maybe they were wanted him alive so if the police found out about the business they could blame everything on him and let him take the biggest fall.

Because Moriggi had died from the beating. They'd lucked out there, in several ways. The big Italian had had a reputation for getting in fights and holding and inspiring grudges. The three of them weren't even suspected, or at the most were just names on a big list of suspects. In the confusion, they hadn't taken the bastard's money, so while robbery could've been a motive, a vendetta looked just as likely. He, Deuce and Fred hadn't even been questioned. Now it was unlikely he'd ever be suspected. More than a year had gone by, and few people missed Moriggi. Deuce had gotten scared and blown the town a few weeks after the mugging. Fred had gotten scared and left as well, when he'd found out Blaine had just gotten his sight back. Fred had pretty much cut him out after the mugging and his injury, had had as little to do with Blaine as possible. That business about old scores worked both ways, after all.

Almost from the moment Blaine had learned he'd been blinded by the blows, he'd cursed Moriggi to hell. It hadn't mattered that the guy had already paid for what he'd done with his life. It hadn't mattered that Blaine had never been in a church in his life, that until recently he hadn't cared enough about religion to even count as an atheist. With every day, as Blaine had to contend with the darkness, the limits, the helplessness, and the growing boredom and frustration, he'd wished eternal damnation with all his heart and soul on the guy who'd done this to him. Even now he couldn't believe he'd brought the blindness on himself. Moriggi had been involved in the illegal enterprise which had made him such a vulnerable target. Moriggi had idiotically tried to play macho and provoked the beating. Moriggi had struck the blow that had taken his sight. Blaine had wished the worst fates he could imagine on the man he'd thought doubly beyond his reach, both by death and by his own helplessness.

And somehow, Blaine had gotten his wish. Moriggi *had* gone to hell. Most likely it was because of earlier things he'd done in his life, with fighting and blinding Blaine merely the last entry in a big book of complaints about him. But perhaps Blaine was responsible for Moriggi being in hell, since his try at a mugging had caused Moriggi's death and provoked the final sins that had brought the guy there. Blaine would have liked to think his curse had something to do with it as well, simply out of the bitter memories of his year of darkness, a darkness he'd thought was going to last a lot longer. However, he really doubted God listened to people's curses. He knew the old stories about people who were denied heaven because they'd been cursed by their parents, or local priests, or their angry girlfriends. Even he had to admit that lacked justice, somebody suffering for eternity because someone had cursed them while in a tantrum, often someone who'd acted even worse in the business than they had. Blaine recalled his own dad, throwing a fit every time he'd caught him reading a book, finally beating the crap out of him and ordering him out of the house over money he'd never even seen, let alone taken. His old man had goddamned him often enough, despite loudly not believing in any of this himself, especially when a few days after the business over the money, Blaine had gotten himself full of liquid courage, gone back, jumped the old bastard and beaten *him* up for a change. Too many people would be damned if curses worked.

So he doubted it was the curse . . . unless . . . somehow this made Blaine uncomfortable . . . what if his curse had been the final straw that had broken the camel's back? That last, infinitesimal little push that had sent Moriggi to hell instead of heaven. Which would mean he was a lot more responsible for Moriggi's damnation than if he'd just killed him. Which might explain why he could see into hell through the bastard's eyes now.

Because, when Moriggi had gone to hell with his curse, he'd taken Blaine's eyes with him. All right, you could call it symbolic, you could call it superstitious, you could say it wasn't how it literally happened . . . Moriggi and Blaine's sight both went to hell together, and both due to the same incident. Blaine's eyes had been in hell for a year, and now that he could see again, he could see hell . . . through the eyes of the man he'd sent there.

Which left Blaine with a problem. As far as he was concerned, Moriggi could stay in hell. He'd deserved it, after all, and anyone could see the place wasn't as bad as those hell-and-damnation preaching clowns made out. But Blaine knew his visits to the afterlife were killing him, and he wasn't ready to go there permanently yet. He was afraid to close his eyes for any length of time, he was lucky to get any sleep at all at night, and the fear that miserable place caused him every time he went there was twisting his guts, making him ill. The doctor was already on his case about his blood pressure. And Blaine knew he was going to need his health soon. The end to his disability benefits was in sight; he was going to have to either find a job or get a new

racket soon.

So he had to sever whatever tie he had with Moriggi and fast, before his glimpses of hell wrecked him. How, he didn't know; all he knew was it had to be done. He'd regained his sight, and he wasn't going to regain it only to enjoy it for however many months he'd have before this business broke his health. He'd do whatever it took.

Blaine was now doing whatever it took. He was sitting in a chair with his eyes closed. He was also wandering through the desolate city now, looking through Moriggi's eyes. These new trips were worse than the old. Now that he knew where he was, the dreary city seemed even more unwelcoming to him . . . and a lot more frightening. And where before he could open his eyes and escape, he now had to keep them closed and stay there in the hopes of seeing some detail that would allow his escape from Moriggi. The knowledge that escape was just a single movement away and he couldn't take it was a torment to Blaine.

He'd made three of these prolonged trips of exploration so far, staying as long as he could absolutely stand it. So far he'd seen no details other than the ones he'd seen on his earlier trips there. This dead-end hell was getting at least as repulsive to him as the pool of burning sulfur or the torture chamber the place was supposed to be. If he ever got away from here, Blaine was going to work hard at not going back. Problem was, he didn't know any good way to duck this place. Reforming wouldn't really count, as he'd had to give up his rackets when he'd been blinded and, despite staying in shape, he didn't really feel like going back into them and taking the risk. Repenting and getting religion probably wouldn't work. God was no dope. He'd know Blaine didn't really feel guilty about any of his earlier crimes. For example, he was still glad he'd killed that bastard Moriggi and that the creep was currently wandering aimlessly in hell. If you accepted there was a hell, you pretty much had to accept there was a God who knew when somebody was truly repenting and who was pretending out of fear of the consequences. Perhaps Blaine's best bet would be to just take care of himself and get so old he got totally senile, and wouldn't know or care where he was, or even if he was dead or alive.

Anyhow, he had to stop visiting hell first before he could worry about staying out of there.

He looked around. Nothing unusual. Just the usual wiped-out, sickly people, dismal buildings, dirty streets, garbage, and the eternal night. Nothing he could see that could help him.

Then, up ahead, he saw the crowds draw back. He knew what it had to be. Only the Door would bring any kind of reaction from those people. He could tell where it was, by the way the people were backing away and taking the long way around. He'd never seen anybody actually run in hell. Even the scary Door couldn't get that much of a reaction from these basket-cases.

Damn, Moriggi wasn't going to walk around the Door on the far side of the street, he was turning away from it, picking a different route to go. No! He wanted to see that damn Door, even if Moriggi didn't want to look at it. The hell with what that bastard wanted anyhow! It was *his* fault they were both there!

Blaine tried then to will Moriggi to turn around and go toward the Door. He could see through his eyes, couldn't he? Why shouldn't he be able to control his body? All right, it was technically his soul, not his body, but Moriggi had been so passive up to now Blaine ought to be able to control him. Why didn't any of the dead get mad? Rant, rave, go beat up the wimpier sinners? Was this part of their punishment? They misused their anger and courage in life, so now they had no strength or rage to fall back on when things got bad? But why wouldn't Moriggi obey *his* will, then?

It was like Moriggi was the living person, and Blaine was the ghost. He couldn't touch anything, he saw only through Moriggi's eyes, heard only what he heard and nobody noticed him. Even Moriggi, who must have held a grudge for what had been done to him, didn't know he was there.

"*Notice me, asshole!*" Blaine yelled in frustration.

It was then that Moriggi froze in his tracks. Blaine didn't have to feel to know his host had gone absolutely rigid. He could tell just by the way he saw the man's body freeze.

Speaking? But Blaine knew he'd tried speaking before when he had visions of the underworld, and hadn't been able to do it. Why should he be able to shout now? Wait! That had been his own voice, not Moriggi's. He had been trying to speak through his host's mouth before, not his own. This time he'd shouted out in rage for real. The voice had come from his own body, despite him keeping his eyes shut. And somehow, despite Moriggi and him being separated by God-knew-what, the guy had heard him.

Blaine felt an icy chill run through him, felt a coldness, an emptiness. It didn't matter he was nice and safe in his apartment and just seeing into hell, he felt it. As if his life . . . his strength . . . *something* . . . was being drained out of him.

Moriggi, on the other hand, seemed more alive than anyone else Blaine had seen down there. Even though Blaine could only get glimpes of the man whose eyes he was seeing through, the man was tensed up, turning around, looking for Blaine.

"Where are ya'?!" Moriggi was yelling, dukes up and ready for a fight. "Where are ya', goddamnit!?"

That Moriggi had suddenly come alive again was strange enough, but his condition seemed catching. Instead of stampeding away from him, the other dead were clustering around him, ignoring the fact they could easily be on the receiving end of the angry man's fists. Blaine caught signs of new interest and life on all the people's faces there, no longer burned-out druggies.

In fact, Moriggi in his anger and the others in their curiosity even forgot their fear of the Door. Blaine suddenly remembered why he was visiting in the first place and looked for the Door.

As Moriggi twisted around, Blaine caught a glimpse of the Door. It was a huge, imposing thing, shaped like the door to one of those old, big churches. It seemed to be made of black wood, not iron like he'd first thought. Wasn't hell supposed to have iron doors? He recalled reading that somewhere. Well, it seemed to be reinforced with iron. And on the Door were letters. . . . Blaine willed Moriggi to turn so he could read them. Moriggi didn't seem to respond to Blaine's urging, but happened to turn so Blaine got a look at the sign. Reading the big letters turned out be easy. They were carved right above the Door, and read:

THE DOOR OF MERCY

Mercy? In hell? If the door led to mercy, then why did the damned shun it? They needed all the mercy they could get. And anyway, weren't they all supposed to be stuck there for good?

Never mind that mystery. Silva seemed to know something about the Door; Blaine would put the question to him tomorrow. Right now he had to get out of there. Something was sucking the strength out of him. He felt weak; he felt sick. Bad as hell was, it had never affected him like this before.

Blaine opened his eyes. It took a lot more effort than he expected; it was a struggle. For a brief moment, it seemed like he didn't have the strength even to do that.

Then they were opened again, and Blaine was back safe in his own apartment. Well, as safe as he could be. He felt like half the life had been drained out of him. He felt empty and nauseous all at once. Every one of his muscles ached, as if he'd been working long and hard. Even his mind felt blurred and tired.

All Blaine wanted to do was go to bed and sleep for a century, and to even do that he had to wait until he was strong enough and got up the willpower to get out of his chair.

"The Door of Mercy," said Silva when he heard the description. "From the Hans Anderson story. But then again your version of hell does more closely resemble the Anderson story's version than the traditional fire pit."

"What was the story about?" asked Blaine, already feeling uncomfortable. He had told Silva as much about his last visit down there as he dared. He admitted he thought he was linked to somebody he'd held a grudge against down there, but said he couldn't guess who it was, as he'd been in a lot of fights during his life. It could even have been his father, who he hadn't seen since that business over the

missing money back when he was sixteen, and so could be dead. A plausible story, anyhow. Silva seemed to believe it, which was just as well.

"It's in this old fairy tale about a bratty little girl who drowns and goes to hell," said the would-be sorcerer. "I kinda thought they were too tough with her: she was a snotty kid, but drowning should'a been enough to have taught her a lesson. Anyhow, there's the Door of Mercy down there, too. One day the kid hears her mother mourning for her up on earth, feels guilty about the bad things she's done, and the Door opens. So she goes to heaven."

"So why don't the people down there run for that Door whenever it appears?" demanded Blaine. "Why do they run from it like it was the door to the police station?"

"All sorts of reasons," said Silva. "This might not be like the door in the story. Maybe it leads only to oblivion . . . annihilation . . . true death. That would be a mercy next to the existence they lead in that city. Or maybe the Door only leads to reincarnation, like the Indians and Chinese believe in. A chance to live a whole 'nother life with all of life's problems and maybe end up back in hell when you're done. Or the Door could be just a cruel trick somebody down there is playing. For that matter, in the story, it was locked most of the time. If you were down there, would you want to even try that Door and find it was locked? A disappointment beyond anything you've ever experienced in life. And finally, you descibed the people down there as whipped and hopeless. Maybe they've been hit by so many things . . . their lives, their deaths, a bad afterlife . . . that they're afraid of any more changes, no matter how good they might be. Don't both good and bad people up here end up scared of change after being hit with enough of them?"

Blaine could only nod.

"But why did I feel weak and drained when Moriggi noticed me?" he asked. "It was like my strength went into him and the people near him. I got so weak I felt sick and the others acted like they were alive again."

"The scary thing is, that does jive with a lot of the old descriptions of the afterlife," explained Silva. "The dead wouldn't show much life or personality until they got a taste of life, then some of their old character would return. In the Greek myths, the spirits of the dead became like their old selves when they were given animal blood to drink — they absorbed a little life from the blood. And lots of those "weird but true" books tell stories about ghosts that drain the life and vitality out of their victims the way a vampire sucks blood."

Blaine had suspected as much, but he still didn't like hearing it.

"You mean if they realize I'm visiting hell, those dead bastards could suck the life out of me? Kill me?"

"Pretty easily. From your description, they didn't even

purposely try to drain your life, it just happened, once you communicated with your old enemy," said Silva. "Problem is, that life draining might give you your chance to sever ties with your enemy and get away from there for good . . . or at least until you die."

"Oh, how's that?"

"When he got your energy, he got mad, became active instead of passive. Even forgot his fear of the Door of Mercy. So if you could somehow convince him to try the Door while he was still acting like he was alive and had a will of his own, he might do it. You said he could hear you."

"But I risk gettin' all my life sucked outta me and endin' up down there with him forever," grumbled Blaine. "Besides, how am I gonna get that guy to listen to me? We hated each other's guts when he was alive. He blew up even after more than a . . . after all these years. How can I talk him into goin' through a door he's scared of?"

Silva could only shrug.

"I don't know what you can say to him. You knew this guy, I didn't. Maybe you could forgive him for whatever he did to you, or even apologize for what happened between you two. Or if that doesn't work, maybe you can trick him into goin' through the Door. Say you're waiting for him on the other side, you could fight it out then. Or dare him to go through the Door: if he was macho durin' his lifetime, that might work."

"And will I get loose from him? Can you guarantee I won't be linked to this guy's spirit any more?"

"If the devil hasn't put some fake Doors of Mercy up to bust people's chops, it should. If his spirit is annihilated, he'd be at real rest and you'd never hear from him again. If he goes on to reincarnation or even heaven, any debts between you and him should be settled and the tie severed. And if you still end up with him when you close your eyes, well, wouldn't you rather visit heaven than hell? By the looks of you, visiting hell sure hasn't done you much good!"

Blaine flinched at the reminder of his appearance. Like the stooge in some of the spook stories he'd read back in his younger days, his adventures in the afterworld were telling on him. He looked haggard, he'd lost his appetite and weight, he had aged visibly over the past several weeks. He hated the plan Silva was suggesting, hated the risk to himself, hated letting Moriggi off the hook after all the trouble the bastard had caused him . . . but if he didn't try it, this was going to wreck his health, maybe even kill him. Blaine felt his year in darkness had evened the score for about every crime he'd ever committed, considering how so many of the people he'd victimized had either asked for it or left themselves so wide open someone else would've got them if he hadn't. He didn't deserve death and hell besides.

"I've got to think hard on this," he said, stalling the decision he knew was inevitable. "Seems awfully risky. But I'll tell you what I've decided. And if I try it, I'll tell you what happens."

If I'm alive after I try it, Blaine thought. *And if I don't end up coming after you with a knife because your fool idea nearly got me killed . . . or if it doesn't work. If it saves me, Silva, I'll be your friend for life, but if it doesn't, I'll have nothing to lose getting you before Moriggi drags me down.*

It was as he turned to leave that Blaine noticed the emptied shelves in Silva's room. It was where Silva had kept his books on magic and various magician type doodads like statues and crystals and plaques with hexagrams engraved on them.

"What, ya get robbed?" Blaine asked, stabbing a finger in the general direction.

"I crated them up and put them in my closet," Silva explained. "I may be throwing them out or giving them away, but I haven't decided yet. All these years I've been hopin' to find something that actually worked, that I could really believe in. I think that started meaning more to me than gettin' rich or successful by magic, just to find something I believed in. You managed to convince me you were visitin' hell, you have me actually believin' you. So the main thing you're supposed to do if you believe in hell is try t' stay outta it. I'm gonna find a church an' try that for a while. And most of those churches don't think sorcery's a good idea. So I'm givin' it up . . . at least until I see if plain old-fashioned religion is any better."

Things were finally coming together, Blaine realized. After five weeks and more than twenty frustrating trips to hell, he'd finally been with Moriggi when the guy encountered the Door of Mercy again. He had Moriggi where he wanted him, and he knew what to do.

All he needed now was the courage.

He knew once he spoke aloud and Moriggi noticed him, he'd start draining him again. Nothing like that had happened on his other visits to hell. Even after that first time, Blaine apparently had to get the damned's attention to be open to that attack. But memory of that first time, the horrible weakness he'd experienced, stayed with him. Also these trips to hell since then had taken a lot out of him. Before, Blaine had left in a hurry. These later visits he'd had to stay to look for the Door. He'd kept his eyes closed and made himself stay until he was close to screaming to be let out. Each time, summoning up the willpower to make himself go back, make himself stay, got harder.

The first time the drain had hit him, this business had already been wearing on him, but he was sure he had a lot more reserves of strength then than he had now.

But if he didn't do it now, when was he going to do it? It was wiping him out. He already looked like somebody you'd expect to meet in a rehab center. Didn't dare let it go on any longer. *He'd* be one of the ones down here, wandering the streets and muttering uselessly to himself. Better to lead Moriggi to annhilation, or even to heaven, than that. If he couldn't stay out of hell permanently, at least let him put it off a couple decades!

Well, if he was going to do it, at least he could do it with a little style. No way was he going to go to Moriggi cap in hand and beg him to go through that door, do that or pitch that forgivness routine to him, not unless he absolutely had to. It was Moriggi's fault they were both in this place, and he'd treat him as such.

"Hey, *stupid*!" Blaine yelled, nearly losing contact with Moriggi as his eyelids suddenly strained to pop open. "Been lookin' for me?"

As before, Blaine felt his strength leech out of him as Moriggi started acting alive and aware again. This time, however, Moriggi was less belligerent than last time. Oh, he had his fists up, and he acted mad, but unlike last time, he acted sorry for himself as well.

"Where are you?" Moriggi demanded, looking around. "Haven't you done enough to me? You *killed* me, f' Christsake! I'm *here*. Why do ya' gotta come around tormentin' me as well? Ain't you effin' satisfied yet?"

How Moriggi recognized the man who had killed him from the sound of his voice was something Blaine didn't understand. They'd only met on that fateful night, and while Blaine had known Moriggi's name from his list of targets, he couldn't think of any way his victim could've learned his. Even if Saint Peter had told him who'd done him in, how could he recognize a voice he'd only heard once after more than a year? Well, Blaine supposed since only his eyes had been to hell, he shouldn't be able to *hear* what Moriggi was saying, either, but there he was.

"Don't lip me, ya dumb fuck!" yelled Blaine, wanting to keep on top of the situation, no matter how ill he was feeling. "Remember what I did t' ya the last time ya tried t' get tough with me."

"Ya wanna try it again?" growled Moriggi. "Come on out an' try it! Or don't ya got your two friends with ya this time? Ya need them t' take me on, don't ya?"

"Like a dumb shit like you scares me," growled Blaine, aware of the crowd their macho act was drawing. "I've seen ya. I've seen ya walkin' down the street, right past the door outta hell. Ya never even had guts enough t' try it."

The dead man's usually pale face went red with both shame and rage.

"We all try that goddamn door when we get here! It's always locked!" Moriggi snarled.

Blaine had to stifle a groan. He'd forgotten about that possiblity! But he wouldn't give up and get out just yet. Too much was riding on him getting the creep through the door.

"Yeah," he said, as sarcastic as he could. "And have ya tried it lately? I've never seen ya' ever try the door once! What's a matter, Moriggi? Lose your balls when they sent ya' here?"

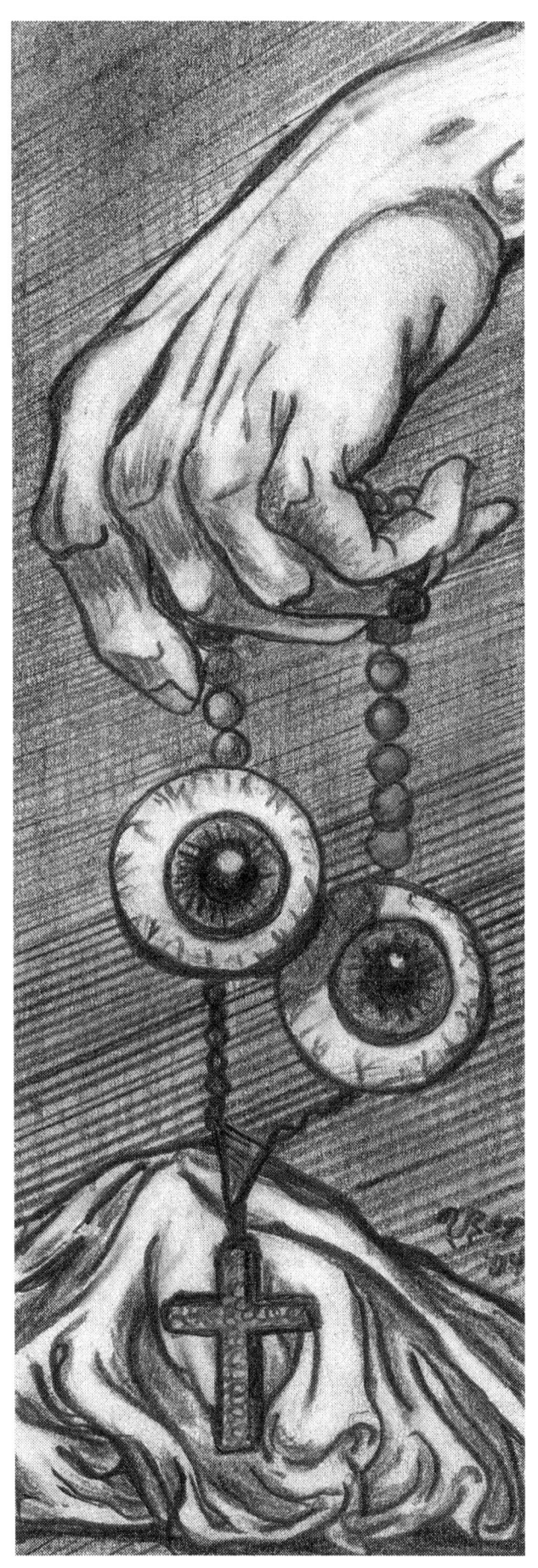

BY CHARLES GAROFALO

Blaine wished he could feel as tough as he sounded. Like before, he felt all the life and strength being squeezed out of him like water out of a sponge. He had to get the asshole through the Door and fast.

"What are ya?" he demanded, trying to sound as nasty as possible. "Scared? Yellow? Chicken?"

"That door won't *open*, damn you!" snarled Moriggi, not considering he was hardly in the position to damn anybody. "Look, I'll show ya! Just a fake they've put up to make sure we stay miserable!"

Actually, right now he looked more miserable than angry and defiant, but he was heading for the door to prove his point.

Moriggi grabbed the huge Door's latch and pulled. It wasn't the sort of half-hearted tug a person insisting he "couldn't do" something often delivered. Moriggi had the latch in both hands and was clearly pulling with all his strength. Blaine couldn't see his face, looking through the guy's eyes at his tensed and straining arms. He felt sure Moriggi's ugly face, despite being dead, was glowing red with the effort. He might've started out just trying to show Blaine the job was impossible, but now he was really struggling with the Door. He wanted out. They all wanted out. Blaine could see the longing on all the damned faces out of the corner of Moriggi's eye. Now that their apathy was temporarily gone due to the life they were taking from him, they wanted out of this dead-end world, too. None of them moved to help Moriggi, though. Maybe there were rules against helping someone working on the Door. Or maybe they were just afraid of being disappointed one more time.

Still, for all the effort, this was no good. Blaine couldn't afford to lose much more strength, and Moriggi was getting nowhere with the Door. He had to be pushed to do more!

"Come on, ya' goddamn pantywaist! Put your back into it!" he yelled.

No, that wasn't working. Moriggi was tugging at the Door with all his strength, still, sweating over it, but Blaine could see he was getting discouraged. Losing hope. Soon he'd give up on the Door . . .

Blaine didn't want to say what he had to say next. Every part of him rebelled at the idea of it. Moriggi deserved his fate, he'd be coming after the bastard with a gun right now if he'd lived through that business a year ago. But Moriggi was pulling him down to hell with him. Blaine couldn't take it.

"Moriggi," he said, and this time his voice came out choked and weak. It was no act, his strength was being drained to the point that he could no longer shout loud. Not to mention he loathed what he was about to say. But he actually did now sound sad and contrite, which was important. It might have been even better if he'd felt any remorse over what he'd done, but he'd settle for sounding

like he did.

"Moriggi," Blaine continued. "I'm . . . sorry for what I did to you a year ago."

Blaine felt he would rather have that real acid vomit in his mouth just then than those words, but they seemed to work. *Almost* work, anyhow. He could see the Door actually give a bit, maybe a tiny bit, a quarter inch or so, without actually opening. Almost open, but not even a crack in which you could see the other side.

This encouraged Moriggi, who now struggled with the Door with renewed effort, as his fellow dead now drew closer and actually started to shout encouraging things. But it wasn't good enough for Blaine. He had to get the Door open and Moriggi through it before they either drained all his strength and killed him, or he lost courage and forced his eyes open to escape from here.

"Lou. It *is* Lou, ain't it?" Blaine said, and the words were even harder to say than the apology had been. "I forgive you for giving me that concussion and blinding me! And may God forgive you any other sins you may have comitted."

There, it was out. A perfectly insincere forgiveness that, Blaine thought, was only words, not actually meant, for how could he forgive? But it was out. And it worked. Because, when he heard that, Moriggi gathered up all his strength and gave the Door one last great pull. And the Door flew open.

Light dazzled Blaine, pure white, blinding light, like the sun, or an arc light. As his host Moriggi closed his eyes, Blaine tried to make his open. He had no idea what the source of the light was, whether it was the light they supposedly had in heaven, or the light from the flames of the classic fire-and-brimstone Hades, but whatever it was, he didn't want to accompany Moriggi on his last trip and experience whatever he did. That really might finish him.

Blaine found his eyes wouldn't open. The light seemed to have returned much of the strength he'd just had drained from him, but his eyelids refused to respond to his command. It was like he was paralyzed: not only wouldn't the muscles in his face respond, he couldn't even lift his hands to try to force the eyelids open. And Moriggi, still dazzled, still probably weak from his efforts, was stumbling through the Door.

Blaine struggled to escape, yelling and cursing, knowing he was sitting in his room but also facing something that was unknown and frightening. He screamed, he swore, he blamed everybody for his fate, starting with Moriggi and working his way up through his parents and friends and finally ending up with God. This had all been a deliberate trap, set to catch him!

He had no idea what was going on. The light dazzled him, he couldn't see where Moriggi was heading. He couldn't tell if the Door of Mercy slammed shut behind him or if everyone who'd been nearby was following

Moriggi into whatever came next. Blaine hoped not. He figured that forgiving his enemy and repenting his sin were probably pluses in Saint Peter's book for him, but he didn't think they'd appreciate him bringing a whole block full of down-and-out bums from the pit into heaven. Wetbacks swimming across the River Styx. He'd read whatever the local libraries had about hell, once Silva had come up with his theory, although Milton's and Dante's long poems had proven too much for him. He recalled reading that between the crucifixion and the resurrection Jesus was supposed to have visited hell and let a lot of people from the Old Testament out of it. Blaine felt God would be less than thrilled to find a lowlife like him matching one of his son's really great feats.

Blaine's, or rather Moriggi's, eyes had managed to get used to the light. Blaine could now see through his eyes, into what must be heaven.

It was only a glimpse, only the briefest glimpse of what lay on the other side. People who'd nearly died came back with far more detailed stories of what was there. But Blaine saw, even if he didn't understand, something more beautiful by far than anything he'd ever seen in his life in that one blurred glimpse. Something so beautiful as to make all his past life look uglier than hell had been by comparison. An incredible beauty that would haunt him for the rest of his life and highlight all the crimes he'd done in such a way that Blaine could never ignore them, or their ugliness, ever again.

What a concussion and a year of blindness hadn't been able to do, what all his trips to hell hadn't done, this one moment near heaven managed. The paralyisis holding Blaine disappeared and his eyes flew open.

Blaine knew he'd never see the afterworld again until he died like any normal person. And a broken, frightened young man, haunted by guilt he'd never imagined and beauty he still couldn't conceive, sat staring at the dingy little apartment which was his mortal home.

Blaine now found himself in the grip of a new obsession. Seemed like nothing would satisfy him. Now he could close his eyes and see nothing but the black or red insides of his lids, and that's what he'd wanted for these long months. The way he had looked forward to it, it would seem like heaven just to see nothing! Just to be without his forced visions of hell! But now that he had seen the flooding daylight from behind the Door of Mercy, well, he could only say that seeing nothing when he shut his eyes was itself like hell! He had to have another vision of the glory he had never imagined, the glory that lucky stiff Moriggi was enjoying twenty-four hours a day! That is, if they even had days there! Or wasn't it all one big day? Seems like he had read that someplace.

He made his way back to Silva's apartment reluctantly and told him the whole story, this time with no omissions.

The other man was not particularly surprised at the criminal elements; you couldn't even be acquainted with Blaine for more than ten minutes without starting to suspect something. What surprised Silva the most, he admitted, was just how right his guess about the Door had been. And that he was now inclined to chalk up to "the Lord's guidance."

And that's what Blaine wanted more of. But Silva, newly religious, was now more careful in handing out spiritual advice. He referred Blaine to the pros: "Why dontcha go to a priest and tell your story? Maybe he'll know what to suggest — beyond the obvious, I mean. Why can't you just mend your ways and hope for the best like the rest of us slobs? When your time's up, maybe there'll be a place in heaven for you."

Blaine's dismissive hand-wave signaled that he'd thought of that — and rejected it — long ago. Not good enough. He couldn't wait! But he knew if he tried to hasten the process by, say, shooting himself, he'd ruin the whole thing. The Almighty didn't look kindly at suicide, or so he'd heard all his life. Like you were giving up on any life-raft God might toss you. And besides, who was he kidding? He'd never be able to repent. He liked his sins, and he sure wasn't sorry for the worst of the ones he'd committed. No ticket to heaven that way. But there was something in Silva's words that stayed with him. Maybe a priest was the answer.

Father O'Fagan, shifting in his desk chair to keep his butt awake, finished listening to Blaine's whole fantastic story. His expert opinion was to put it down to guilt and hallucinations. He had already assured him of priestly confidentiality, so Blaine needn't worry about him going to the cops. The white-haired old man seemed at least a bit shaken by the details both of his criminal life and his visions. He didn't quite know what to say. It was risky telling someone they were becoming too religious for their own good. From the sound of it, fanaticism might be just what poor Blaine needed. To stall for time, the priest asked him:

"But why, my son, have you come to *me* with this story? What can I do for you?"

"Plenty," said Blaine. "Y'see, I figure what I need to do to see the inside of heaven again is to link up with somebody there, just like I did in hell. I don't mean to go blind again, but I think I found a way to take care of that, making sure I can see what's on the other side. This time, see, I need a saint, a holy person, to go to heaven and to take me along, remote control, so's I can see through *his* eyes!" At this point, Blaine reached for his switchblade and started to rise. "That's where you come in. Now just hold still, padre…"

Blaine's eyes had deteriorated since he'd regained his sight; that was true enough. He needn't lie about it, or about the weird ordeal that had probably caused the weakening. Where his ingenuity came in was making up something good about how he came to be in possession of the spare pair of eyes he brought with him to the Mexican doctor. Something about a dying grandfather's bequest. Blaine had the feeling the doc didn't want to look into the matter too closely.

You don't want to know what Blaine, in his desperation, did to get the money for the operation. But he got it, and the day came. He hoped the anesthesiologist knew what the hell he was doing, and that was his last thought as he slipped into the sea of forgetfulness.

He awoke the requisite number of hours later with a hell of a headache. Ordinarily a man in his position would be itching, literally as well as figuratively, to get the bandages off and open his peepers. But Blaine didn't need to unwind the gauze to tell if his experiment was a success. The inside of his eyelids were the screen his feature would play on.

It had worked. Or had it? Blaine pitched sideways in the bed, flinching, recoiling as if to avoid blows left and right. The orderly came a' running to see what could possibly be wrong. Nothing Blaine said before they sedated him made

any sense. But if you knew the back-story, it would have. Seems he was commenting at the top of his lungs about the lava and flames he was seeing, seeing with no escape, not till they doped him up, that is. As he drifted off again, Blaine realized the truth: he was seeing through the transplanted eyes of the priest he had murdered — only who'd have guessed the old bastard was one of those child molesting priests? Now Blaine was stuck with him in the *real* hell, the one old Dante had seen, the one whose only door said:

ABANDON HOPE, ALL YE THAT ENTER HERE.

Charles Garofalo's short tales of horror, many with a pronounced Robert Bloch influence, have appeared in Weirdbook, Eldrich Blue, 100 Creepy Little Creature Stories, *and* 100 Vicious Little Vampire Stories. *His hobby is collecting hobbies, including books, old movies, horror, classical music, art, animated cartoons, comics, and nature hikes.*

THE CAULDRON

We enjoy letters from our readers! Drop the editor an email at <criticus@aol.com> with your comments on this issue . . . and you may find a reply in the next issue's letter column! All letters become the property of Strange Tales *and may be edited for publication.*

*　　　*　　　*

I was trying to find submission guidelines for *Strange Tales* on your website, but could only find guidelines for submitting books. Can you please direct me to where I could find this information?

Thank you for your time.

Ian Rogers

*　　　*　　　*

Strange Tales *is not always an open market; please query the editor at <criticus@aol.com> to find out if he is currently reading, or watch the message boards at www.wildsidepress.com for more information.*

"Fire burn and cauldron bubble"

This is the original logo for "The Cauldron"